ALSO BY
LISI HARRISON

FOR MIDDLE-GRADE READERS

The Clique series
The Alphas series
The Girl Stuff series

FOR YOUNG ADULTS

The Monster High series
The Pretenders series

THE Pack

LISI HARRISON

A YEARLING BOOK

Text copyright © 2021 by Lisi Harrison
Cover art copyright © 2021 by Luke Lucas

All rights reserved. Published in the United States by Yearling, an imprint of Random House Children's Books, a division of Penguin Random House LLC, New York. Originally published in hardcover in the United States by Delacorte Press, an imprint of Random House Children's Books, a division of Penguin Random House LLC, New York, in 2021.

Yearling and the jumping horse design are registered trademarks of Penguin Random House LLC.

Visit us on the Web! rhcbooks.com

Educators and librarians, for a variety of teaching tools, visit us at RHTeachersLibrarians.com

Library of Congress Cataloging-in-Publication Data is available upon request.
ISBN 978-0-593-18070-9 (trade) — ISBN 978-0-593-18071-6 (ebook) — ISBN 978-0-593-18072-3 (pbk.)

Printed in the United States of America
10 9 8 7 6 5 4 3 2 1
First Yearling Edition 2022

This novel is for the wild creature that lives
inside of you. Some days you will hear her roar.
Other days she will purr. Pay attention either way.
She knows you better than anyone.

one

Charm House, the old convent that had been converted into a boarding school for girls, was the last place Sadie Samson thought she'd find herself on a Friday afternoon— or ever.

The stone institution was at the edge of the forest, where brittle leaves lay in forgotten piles by the iron gates. It had a spindly bell tower jutting up from its center like a murder weapon, and the Virgin Mary statue above the entrance was missing an arm. So, yeah. The whole scene was beyond the scope of Sadie's imagination. And yet there she was, seated in a dimly lit office across from a woman roughly her grandmother's age, with a strict silver bob, red-framed glasses, and a nameplate that read *Headmistress Flora*. Outside, rain streaked down the arched windowpanes like tears.

"Do you know why you've been transferred to Charm House?" Miss Flora asked, without the tiniest bit of a British accent. This, too, was unimaginable. In the movies, headmistresses always had accents, especially at charm schools.

They also had permanent scowls, thin lips, and beady eyes that could see straight into a girl's soul.

But Miss Flora spoke the way everyone else in Timor Lake, Washington, spoke: *bag* sounded like *beg; leg* sounded like *lig;* and *keg* sounded like *cake.*

Why, yes, Miss Flora, I do know why I was transferred to Charm House, Sadie wanted to answer. *I'm here because I'm too weird for middle school and no one wants to be around me, not even my own parents.* But there was no point in saying any of that out loud; hearing it would only make her cry. Because without her parents, Sadie had no one. No siblings, no cousins, no pets. And friends? Friends were for people who fit in— not misfits with dark circles under their eyes, straw-blond hair that grew out instead of down, balloon-animal muscles, a heightened sense of smell, and anger issues. Instead, Sadie shrugged like she didn't know the answer and waited for Miss Flora to fill the silence, the way grown-ups often did.

"According to this report," Miss Flora continued, "on day three at Timor Lake Middle, you were rude and disruptive during a school assembly."

"It was an accident," Sadie insisted. "I didn't mean to—"

"How was snoring while a firefighter shared safety procedures an *accident*?"

"I have trouble sleeping at night, so I get really tired during the—"

"And what about the Coach Frailey incident on day thirteen?"

"She told me to run."

"And run you did." Miss Flora peered over the rims of her glasses. "Two hundred meters in twenty-six seconds, is that right?"

"Yes."

"That's almost a world record."

"It is?" Sadie asked, like it was the first time anyone had told her she ran frighteningly fast. But fast only got her so far.

"How does a girl who can't sleep have the energy to run like that?"

"I don't know." The doctors and therapists didn't know, either. No one did. Because of that, Sadie was banished to a creepy institution—one that trick-or-treaters dared each other to visit on Halloween. One parents threatened to send their daughters to when they didn't behave. But this was not a threat. It was real.

"And just this Monday there was an incident in Language Arts," Miss Flora continued. "Do you remember it?"

Sadie nodded. How could she possibly forget?

She had been rehearsing her oral report for days. Recording it on her phone to make sure she was enunciating. Addressing the mirror to perfect her eye contact. Balling her fists to keep from fidgeting. But no amount of recording, addressing, or balling could have prepared Sadie for the real deal. The rows of expectant faces watching her. The hollow tremble of her voice. The shaking hands. The sweaty pits. The brain that knew every word of her presentation but had suddenly gone blank.

Desperate, Sadie looked down at her quaking iPad and checked her notes. As she did, her bushy hair fell forward and blocked her view. She swiped it away and returned to the screen, but it fell again. And again. And again. It was exactly the kind of embarrassing mishap Sierra Porter and Chloe Whitman lived for.

Sadie saw them smirking before she heard them. But thanks to her peculiar ability to hear things from far away, she was able to pick up on the quietest of whispers. So when Sierra leaned over and muttered "Hairy Poppins," it sounded like a shout. Then came Chloe's giggle, which jackhammered through Sadie's eardrums and shattered her heart.

She wanted to run the way one needs to scratch a bug bite—with unstoppable urgency. Only where could she go? Teachers locked their classroom doors for safety. The windows were lined with protective bars. Like a ferocious animal pacing inside its cage, Sadie was trapped.

It was a familiar feeling. White-hot and blinding, it built and boiled inside Sadie whenever she was mocked. Ruth, her therapist, suggested she give this feeling a name. Make it real so Sadie could reason with it, the way one might deal with a temperamental toddler. She settled on Beast. Sometimes Beast cooperated. Sometimes it behaved. But in that moment, Beast had had enough.

So, did Sadie remember the incident? Um, yeah, she did.

"They called me Hairy Poppins," she told Miss Flora, her throat dry and tight.

"And then?"

"I got angry."

"And then . . ."

"I may have pushed over a few desks."

"And then?"

"I tried to shout *Stop!* Only it didn't come out like a word." Sadie paused at the memory of that primal sound, so thundering it shattered windows and sent students running for their lives. "It was . . . I don't know what it was. . . ."

Miss Flora leaned forward in her chair. She smelled like an exotic faraway land. Like chai tea with extra cinnamon. Maybe it was coming from the vials of amber liquid that lined her bookshelves. The ones marked *L.S. Elixir.*

"Sadie," she began, then removed her red frames. "Do you know why you're *really* here? The *real* reason?"

"Uh . . ." Had there been a few mishaps? Sure. But Sadie didn't deserve this, and when the guidance counselor from Timor Lake Middle School had suggested the transfer, her parents didn't think she deserved it, either. But one hushed phone call from Miss Flora had changed all that. And before

Sadie could promise to try harder, she and her bags had been dropped at the iron gates of Charm House. They swore it wasn't a punishment. They promised it was for the best. They said that they loved her more than anything in the world and that they would visit on parents' weekend. Then they were gone.

"Do *you* know why I'm really here?" Sadie tried, her tears returning.

"Yes."

Sadie shifted in her wooden chair. "Will you . . . tell me?"

The headmistress tap-tap-tapped her clawlike fingernails on the desk, as if contemplating her next move. "Despite what the public has been led to believe," she began, "Charm House isn't a punishment for ill-behaved girls. It's a safe haven. A last resort. A fighting chance at normal."

Sadie scoffed. *Normal?* Was that even possible?

"*Charm* doesn't mean what you think it means," Miss Flora continued. "It's an acronym that stands for Center for Human Animal Reform and Manners."

"Human *animal*?"

She nodded as if *human animal* made all the sense in the world. "The girls at Charm House have a certain . . . light."

"What kind of light?"

"An animal light. For reasons we have yet to fully understand, every student at Charm House has a big, bright animal living inside her. It's an incredibly powerful gift . . . too powerful at times, I'm afraid."

"Which animal is it?"

"There are several, actually. We've counted nineteen different species since the school opened in 1907."

"And you think I'm—"

"Yes."

Sadie shifted in her seat. Was this woman serious? "Which one?" she asked, all too aware of how ridiculous the question sounded. At the same time, how comforting an answer would be. If Sadie was part animal, her wild temper and messed-up sleep patterns would make sense. Her dense muscles, untamed hair, and superhuman speed would mean that she was more than just weird. That none of this was her fault.

"I don't know what glorious light lives inside you . . . yet. We'll have our answers after Monday's Charm Ceremony. All you need to know now is that you're safe."

"Safe? Safe from what?" Sadie asked.

Miss Flora glanced at her locked door. "The Institute of Behavioral Science," she whispered. "Its doctors and scientists have been studying girls like you for decades. They want to know how you got these powers and how to rid you of them."

Sadie drew back her head. "Are the powers bad?"

"Everyone in here thinks they're wonderful. But out there . . ." She rolled her wrist at the rain-streaked windowpanes—or rather, what lay beyond them. "Out there it's different."

Sadie squinted, hoping to spot this elusive threat. Even with her remarkable vision, she only saw iron gates, skeletal tree branches, and fog.

"Most typical humans can't accept that you girls are extraordinary. They want the who, what, where, when, how, and why behind this phenomenon. But in order to find all of this out . . . they need to study you."

"Study us? How?"

"Experimentation. I don't mean to scare you, but—"

"Too late," Sadie said with a shiver.

"Luckily, your parents listened to me and agreed to the transfer. Not all parents do. And they pay a very steep price."

"How did you know about me? How do you know my parents?"

"I used to be a high school principal. I have a few trusted connections in the district. When they suspect that a girl is *different*, they alert me before word gets out."

Sadie began rubbing her throbbing temples. It was all too much.

"If I can get to them before IBS does, I can save them. This is why you must keep this place, our true work, a secret. Our goal is to teach you how to control your animal instincts so you can blend in with the Typicals and live a conventional life."

"Are you sure there's animal light inside me?" Sadie asked.

"Yes, and I have a feeling I know which one it is. But feelings aren't facts." Miss Flora stood. "We'll get the facts on Monday during your Charm Ceremony." There was a knock on the door. "Oh, that must be your roommate."

"Roommate?"

Sadie was an only child. Though her parents had divorced when she was two, neither of them had remarried, so there had never been another kid to get used to. There had never been anyone she had to share *anything* with, let alone a bedroom. What if this girl heard her snore?

"She'll show you around and help you get settled."

A thousand questions filled Sadie's already-full brain. But before she could voice them, a narrow-waisted girl entered the office, wearing a safari-beige jumpsuit, Ugg boots, a fleece jacket, and a yellow fanny pack. Her outfit alone made Sadie sweat. It had to be seventy-five degrees in there.

"I'm Amy Rogers," the girl said, and smiled. Then she grabbed Sadie's wrist with her winter-cold hand. "Come on, roomie." With a slight tug, she led Sadie out of Miss Flora's office and down the dimly lit hallway, to who-knows-where.

two

"**W**elcome to Charm House!" Amy said with tour-guide pride as she escorted Sadie through the cavernous hallways. Overhead, a candelabra's flames flickered, casting stuttering shadows across the uneven stone walls. Somewhere in the distance a waterfall burbled. And the smell! It was a fragrant mix of tropical plants, dewy grass, and jasmine. Sadie could practically taste the rainbow.

"Is this where we *live*?" she asked.

"You'll get used to it. Everyone does."

Everyone? How many human animals were there? And more important, what would they think of the new girl?

"We call this upper floor Sun because it's super warm," Amy said.

She was right about that. The place was rain-forest humid—a frizzy-haired girl's biggest nightmare. Sadie considered lowering the hood on her sweatshirt so she could cool off, but she tightened it instead. Amy seemed nice, but even the nice ones hair-stared, and it was too soon to make a bad first impression.

"Most of my classes are up here," Amy explained. "I need a lot of heat, so I like it." She smiled, but her gray eyes remained fixed and lackluster—the same weak way Sadie smiled whenever her mother asked if she'd had a good day at school.

"Do you like Charm House?" Sadie asked. What she really wanted to know was, *Am I going to be miserable* here, *too?* Because in her experience, school was a place for being mocked and ridiculed. A place where people decided whether you were someone worthy of friendship or someone to avoid. The last place she'd ever want to live.

"I used to."

Without another word, Amy began running her fingernails along the stone walls, lifting them briefly when she encountered a classroom door or a stained-glass window, then placing them back down when the stone returned. Each nail had a thin black stripe of polish painted down the center that was starting to chip and fade. Was that a Charm House trend or an Amy thing? More questions to add to her growing list. A list that included, *Hey, Amy, what animal are you?* But instinct urged Sadie not to pry.

"Why don't you like it here?" Sadie asked instead. "Did something bad happen?"

"The other floors are cooler," Amy said, changing the subject. "Literally. Cave is one level down and is seventy-two degrees, you know, to keep it fair for everyone. That's where we sleep and eat. Oh, and the Watering Hole is there, too. Shade, the level below that, is where the warm-bloods have their classes. It's too chilly down there for me, but you might like it."

"What's the Watering Hole?"

"The spa. Everyone in the Pack thinks—" Amy shook her head as if erasing a thought. "*Some* of the girls here think theming everything after nature is kind of babyish, but"—she lowered her voice and whispered—"I think it's kind of fun."

"The Pack? What's the—"

A gong sounded. Its metallic timbre rattled Sadie's bones and redirected her panic. Was this a call to arms? An earthquake drill? An IBS invasion? "What's happening?"

"Dinnertime. We don't use bells at Charm. A lot of the students have hypersensitive hearing. Since gongs vibrate at a lower frequency, we use them instead. Clapping can also be triggering, so we hiss." Wisps of black hair had slipped from Amy's topknot and now fell around her pale face. "Anyway, we should probably get you some food."

"That's okay, I'm not hungry. You can go without me."

"Nah. I usually skip dinner."

"You do?"

"I'm a slow digester."

"Same," Sadie lied. It was easier than explaining why she associated food with bad news—a feeling that had kicked in that afternoon when her mom had surprised her after school and taken her to the Spotted Owl for a double bacon burger and an Oreo shake. Sadie's mom claimed she was doing it to cheer Sadie up after a difficult week. She also claimed it was perfectly normal for Sadie's dad to join them, even though it was her mom's weekend and her dad *never* joined.

While Sadie had eaten, they'd gone on and on about how sometimes parents had to make tough decisions. How those decisions might feel cruel in the moment, but they were really acts of love.

Whatever.

Sadie had let them ramble. As long as she had fries to dip in her milkshake, she could nod and feign interest. But the moment her fries ran out, so did her patience.

"Can we go now?" she'd asked, not realizing that the next stop wasn't home. It was Charm House, for the *real* surprise.

So, no, Sadie would not be eating tonight. Or any other night, for that matter. Eating was what happened before she'd been abandoned by her parents. And Sadie didn't want to think about that moment ever again. She also wasn't in a hurry to encounter a bunch of girls with odd animal powers. Girls who would definitely notice the wild-haired newbie who had no clue what was living inside her or how it had gotten there.

She followed Amy down a flight of stairs to Cave, where the air was thinner, crisper, and laced with fruity shampoo smells. Similar to Sun, Cave had stone walls, dark floors, and flickering candelabras. But here Moroccan throw rugs gave it a more lived-in, homey feel. So did the handwritten signs on each girl's door, which included *Giraffes Stand Tall, Party Animals Inside,* and *Hyenas with Strong Jaws and Big Bras,* to name a few.

"This is us," Amy said as they approached the second-to-last room on the left. The one with a sticky note on the door handle that read *TRAITOR* in black marker. Amy quickly crumpled it into a tight ball and stuffed it into the pocket of her jumpsuit. Then she removed a key from her yellow fanny pack and aimed it at the lock. She missed, poking the wood instead.

"Are you okay?"

"I can't see very well without my glasses."

"Why aren't you wearing them?" Sadie asked as Amy tried the lock again.

"They always slide off my face because of my moisturizer, so, like, what's the point?"

"How much moisturizer do you wear?"

"A lot." After two more attempts, Amy finally unlocked the door and said, "Home, sweet home."

The room smelled like oranges and clove, just like Amy, and barely fit two narrow beds, two desks, and two dressers. The bed on the right boasted a festive stack of colorful quilts, its headboard decorated with family photographs and birthday cards. The bed on the left held a bald mattress and a bare headboard. Sadie's suitcases, which her parents had secretly packed earlier that day, sat patiently by the closet door like three kids waiting to get picked up after school by a mother who would never come.

Amy flicked a switch. The aluminum rectangle over her bed emitted eye-pinching light.

Sadie shielded her face. "What is that? Should I be wearing sunscreen?"

"A heat lamp." Amy giggled. "Why Miss Flora keeps putting me with warm-bloods is beyond me. But don't worry—we'll make it work."

"Was Kate a warm-blood?" Sadie asked, as if she knew what *warm-blood* even meant. What any of this meant.

"How do you know Kate?"

Sadie pointed at the wall beside the empty bed. The words *Kate sleeps here* had been scratched into the paint.

"Oh, yeah." Amy sighed. "Kate had jaguar light. She was a real marker."

"Was?" Sadie sat on the edge of the mattress. *Her* mattress. After going back and forth between her parents' homes for ten years, she found it weird having one bed. One room. One home. One anything.

"She doesn't go here anymore."

"Did she graduate?"

Amy squirted a hefty dollop of orange-and-clove-scented oil into her palm. It absorbed in seconds. "She was taken last weekend."

"*Taken?* By who?"

"Long story."

Sadie was really starting to sweat. From the heat lamp, yes, but also from all the questions. There were so many of them, they were starting to spill from her pores. "Are you a jaguar, too?"

Amy giggled. "Me? No. I have snake light." She flashed two fang-like teeth on either side of her mouth. "See?"

Sadie stared, speechless. Maybe she'd gotten food poisoning at the Spotted Owl and was trapped in a fever dream. Maybe none of this was real. "Are you . . . are you serious?"

"Oh, I'm serious," Amy said. "If I wasn't, would I be able to do this?" She stretched her arms above her head, arched her back, and grabbed her ankles. Only string cheese could bend like that. "My skeleton is super flexible."

"Impressive," Sadie croaked, her throat as dry as the leaves outside.

"I guess." Amy lifted out of her backward bend with astonishing ease. "But I'd rather be a Typical."

"Can you? I mean, is that even possible?"

"Sort of. There's no cure, but we can learn how to blend in with the Typicals and, you know, live normal lives and stuff."

"And if we can't?"

"Then we're in danger of getting picked up by IBS and being sent to the Thirteenth Floor, where we'll be treated like lab rats. Which is what's happening to Kate right now." Amy sat on her bed and hugged a pillow to her chest. "And everyone thinks it's my fault."

"Your fault? Why?" Sadie asked, remembering the *TRAITOR* sign stuck to their door.

"Long story," Amy said, sighing. Then, "I wonder what you are."

"I . . . I have no idea," Sadie said. "This whole thing is probably a mistake."

"Miss Flora doesn't make mistakes."

"Well, it's not like I'm howling at the moon and shape-shifting or anything."

"Animal light isn't like that," Amy said. "Do you have overwhelming cravings? Inexplicable fits of rage? Superhuman senses? Superhero strength?"

Sadie considered her dense muscles, wild hair, uncontrollable temper, erratic sleep patterns, and intense bacon cravings. But still . . . wasn't that just puberty?

"Miss Flora said I'd find out more on Monday."

"Not unless we figure it out first."

"How?" Sadie asked.

Amy smiled, her top two fangs sharp and exposed. "I have

my ways." She lifted Sadie's suitcases onto her bed. "Now let's unpack and get you settled. Your uniform is hanging in the closet, and you'll get a cloak during your Charm Ceremony."

"Cloak?"

"We all have them. And like it or not, you're one of us now."

A band of smile-shaped warmth rose inside Sadie at the sound of those words. She had never been one of anything before.

For the rest of the evening, she and Amy unpacked and sang Taylor Swift songs. After they turned off the lights and wished each other sweet dreams, Sadie wondered if, maybe, just maybe, Charm House might not be so terrible after all. Because when there are other strange people around, strange stops feeling bad. It feels like belonging.

three

$\mathcal{W}$hen the breakfast gong sounded, Sadie forgot all about the whole food-equals-abandonment thing. The savory smell of cured meat had her awake at 5:30, dressed by 5:37, and salivating by 5:38. Her savage appetite was back—the only thing about that Saturday morning that felt familiar.

The Charm House dining hall was a shock to Sadie's system—the opposite of her mother's tranquil sun-soaked kitchen, where eggs popped, bacon sizzled, and jazz music attempted to ease the suffocating silence. And it was nothing like her dad's, where a sticky doughnut was tossed her way as they raced out the door. Here, food smells blended with the bleachy bite of cleaning products, slippered feet shuffled, and girls mumble-yawned the latest gossip. The Grazing Stations were labeled *Carnivore, Herbivore,* and *Omnivore*—that way each animal light knew where to find her ideal meal. But should she want to stray, the options were endless—all-inclusive, all-you-can-eat, all-good!

Sadie side-eyed the gathering strangers as she and Amy grabbed their forest-green trays. Mostly, to gauge the rhythms and rituals of this new world, but also because these so-called humans were so-called animals, and what did *that* look like? Did they have swishing tails? What about sharp horns? Did they stampede? But so far, Charm House girls were like every other girl Sadie had encountered: prettier, cooler, and not interested in her.

"Why is this place called the Calf?" she asked Amy as they slid their trays along the metal rails. "Is it a play on cows?"

"It's not *calf,* like a baby cow," Amy explained. "It's Caf, like short for *cafeteria*."

"Oh. Right. I *mooo* that," Sadie joked. It had been a while since she'd done that.

Smiling, Amy took a hard-boiled egg from the Carnivore buffet, popped it into her mouth, and swallowed it whole.

Sadie gasped. "Did you just—?"

"I'm part snake, remember? We don't chew."

"Bless you."

"I didn't sneeze. I said, 'We don't chew.'"

"Bless you," Sadie tried again because, come on, "don't chew" sounded exactly like a sneeze.

Amy laughed just as a woman with thick eyebrows and wide amber eyes tapped her on the shoulder. "Miss Rogers, you need to chew."

"Bless you," Amy said with a giggle.

"I didn't sneeze," the woman snipped. "I said, 'You need to chew.'"

"Oh, sorry, Ms. Finkle. I thought—"

"Amy, you've been warned about lazy eating before."

"You're right, I'm sorry. Sometimes I forget."

"That's why you're here," the woman said, softening. "This will become second nature soon enough. Don't give up."

"I won't, Ms. Finkle, thank you," Amy said without the slightest hint of snark. She really was trying.

Next, the woman fixed her glowing wide eyes on Sadie. "I don't see any napkins on your tray, Miss Samson. Domesticated girls use napkins."

"Uh, I was just about to get some."

"Very good." She offered a satisfied blink and then walked away, her Crocs squeaking against the waxed wood floors.

"How did she know my name?" Sadie asked.

"The same way she knew I wasn't chewing. That owl knows everything."

Owl?

Once their trays were filled, Sadie followed Amy into the tunnel-shaped dining hall, where two endlessly long banquet tables stretched forward like train tracks. An arched stained-glass ceiling reflected colorful shapes throughout the room.

"There should be some space at the very end," Amy said,

even though there were plenty of available seats right where they were.

Not that Sadie would ever point that out. The only thing she knew for sure about Charm House was that she knew nothing. Better to do what she always did and leave the leading to someone else.

"Cat kisser," said a thin brunette amid a chorus of kissy meow sounds. She was wearing a pink beanie, matching mittens, and a spiteful glare.

"More like cat-*killer*," said her friend.

Amy's gaze remained forward and fixed, like a seasoned victim who refused to let the bullies bring her down. Then, from the side of her mouth, she muttered, "Reptiles. They think I'm a traitor because I have cat friends." She shook her head. "Correction: *had* cat friends. Whatever. Either way, it's super speciesist."

Then Sadie heard a whisper from across the cafeteria: "Raw-meat alert!"

"New girl? Where?" someone else asked.

The voices were too far away for those around her to register. But not Sadie. Thanks to her supersensitive ears, she heard all the nasty things said behind her back.

"Plate full of bacon. Green hoodie. Walking with the snaitor," said the first girl. They looked at her blankly. "Snake traitor," she clarified.

A third girl giggled. "Looks like a turtle."

"Turtles don't eat bacon, Val."

"Well, hyenas don't eat Froot Loops, Mia, and look at you and Liv."

"Fair enough."

"What do you think she did to get here?"

"Probably mauled a teacher."

"Seriously, Liv? When's the last time a turtle mauled anyone?"

"Fine. Then maybe she's a rhino light, and she's got a horn under that hood."

"Hey," Mia said, "what do you get when you cross a rhino and a garden?"

"What?" Val and Liv asked.

"Squash!"

Sadie tightened her hoodie, hoping to shut out the piercing sound of their yipping laughter.

"Ugh. Who laughs like that?" Sadie asked. It was a rhetorical question, but Amy cocked her head and tried to listen for it anyway.

"I don't hear anything, but if I had to guess, I'd say the hyenas." Then, with a sigh, she added, "They're a bunch of fast-talking, corny-joke-telling, power-hungry meanies. Stay away from them. Unless you're a cat. They're scared of cats. Unless you're a lone cat. Then they'll gang up on you and take you down. Basically, just, you know, stay away from them no matter what light you are."

"Yeah, no problem there," Sadie said, instinctively lowering her gaze. Eye contact was for girls who wanted to get noticed.

"Those ones on the left are monkey lights," Amy said. "They're harmless."

Sadie nodded but didn't dare look up.

"They get the best grades," Amy continued, "but they mess around in class, so they're always getting detention. They sit with the dingoes, who are also smart and way more obedient, so professors love them—"

"Teacher's pets," Sadie joked.

"Ha. Yeah, I never thought of it like that."

Just then, four statuesque creatures with elevated chins, elongated necks, and Kardashian lashes slo-moed by. "Giraffes?" Sadie guessed, joking.

"Yup," Amy grumbled. "They think they're all that."

"They kind of are." Their lips were so lusciously plump that Sadie half expected their faces to tip forward.

Amy finally settled on two seats at the very empty end of the table on the right and began cutting her eggs into bite-sized pieces. Not that Sadie was complaining. The more space between her and the other students, the better.

As Sadie was about to fold a strip of bacon into her mouth, Amy said, "So, when are you going to show me what you've been hiding under that hood?"

"How do you know I'm hiding something?"

Amy cocked her head. "When you have scaly skin, venom-filled fangs, and a rubber-band spine, you know what hiding looks like."

Sadie returned to her bacon.

"Well?"

"Well, what?"

"Are you going to show me or do you plan on sleeping in hoodies until we graduate?"

Sadie glanced around the Caf. Once she was certain no one was watching, she lowered her hood. "Happy?" she asked, bracing for laughter.

But Amy didn't laugh. She didn't reference hay, and she didn't recommend they go hat shopping. She unzipped her fanny pack and handed Sadie a vial of oil.

"ABM," she said. "Always be moisturizing." Then she added, "Run this through your hair a few times a day and you'll never need a hood again."

Sadie rubbed the orange-and-clove-scented oil into her palms and then applied it. "It works!" she said as her brittle strands instantly softened.

"Keep it," Amy told her. "I make a new batch every Friday in Ven Chem." Then, seeing Sadie's confused expression, she added, "Venom Chemistry."

"Thanks." Sadie smiled as she put her hood back on. She trusted Amy. But the other girls? From the sound of it, they didn't even trust each other, so she was far from safe.

"What do we have here?" purred the exotically gorgeous creature who was padding toward them, her emerald-green glare fixed on Sadie. And that hair: butterscotch blond, streaked with black zigzags. She wore a sleeveless bodysuit that showcased her rolling muscles and athletic build. Sadie's physique was similar, but muscles looked different on this girl. They were regal and mighty. Not husky or boyish. It was like how some girls look adorable in sweatpants, while others just look like they have the flu. "I'm guessing you're a panda bear. Those dark under-eye circles are a dead giveaway."

Sadie's insides dipped. She could smell an alpha from two towns over. The scent was unmistakable. Roses and leather. Pride and power. Pretty and tough. Expensive. And this girl reeked of it all.

"She could be a sloth," whispered her friend. She was shorter, less striking. But only when comparing their physical prowess. Her Mohawk boasted the same swirl of colors that her crop top did, making her equally impossible to overlook.

"I'm Lindsey, queen of this jungle," purred the exotic one. "Tiger, obviously." She fingered the choker around her neck— a band of yellow tubular flowers attached to a leather strap. A longer necklace hung below it: a gold chain with a matching gold nail file, which she aimed at her friend. "This is Taylor."

"I'm a chameleon," Taylor added, since Lindsey hadn't bothered.

The girls set down their trays and extended their hands

for an introductory shake. Lindsey's was warm. Taylor's was icy. Both girls had black stripes painted down the center of their fingernails, just like Amy. Only theirs were vibrant, glossy, and fresh, whereas Amy's were chipped and faded.

"I'd introduce you to Kate," Lindsey said, "but Amy got rid of her."

"I did not get rid of her! She was *taken*," Amy snapped, her fangs jutting forward.

"Yes, your plan worked purrfectly."

"Plan?"

"You wanted to get rid of her," Taylor said, "so you made up that bogus attack story."

"Why would I want that?" Amy asked wearily, as if they'd had this conversation dozens of times. "Kate was my best friend."

Lindsey reached for the gold file around her neck and began sharpening her nails into clawlike points. "She was also a cat."

"Meaning?"

"You were jealous."

Amy laughed bitterly. "Why would I be *jealous*?"

"Because Kate is a jaguar, I'm a tiger, and you're a scaly, venomous, cold-blooded reptile—nothing more than a low-lying link in the food chain."

"Um, Linds, as a cold-blooded reptile," Taylor said, "how am I not supposed to be offended by that?"

"Chameleons are totally different, Tay. They're the cats of reptiles. Everyone knows that. And for the record, she's not a sloth, she's a panda," Lindsey continued. "Not just because of the unsightly eye situation, but because my instincts are *never* wrong."

Sadie cut a quick glance to Amy, hoping for some direction. *Should I stand up for myself? Ignore them? Explain that the dark under-eye circles come from a lack of sleep?* But if Amy had an opinion, she kept it between herself and the hash browns she was forking around her plate.

Instead, it was Ms. Finkle who swooped in and saved her. "Lindsey and Taylor, *eat* and *seat* rhyme for a reason. Please stop hovering and find someplace to sit."

"Yes, ma'am," Lindsey said with a smile as fake as her hair color. Then she leaned toward Sadie with a dancer's grace and breathed, "Watch your back, panda. That Amy is a snaky one."

"Yeah, watch your back," Taylor echoed.

Arms linked, they grabbed their trays and strutted past Ms. Finkle, leaving the smell of leather, roses, and intimidation in their wake.

"What was *that*?" Sadie asked, pushing her plate aside. Where were the nice-people schools, and why couldn't her parents have sent her to one of those?

"The Pack," Amy said, scraping off what was left of her black polish. "Don't believe anything they say. They're just trying to turn you against me. They're trying to turn everyone against me."

"Why?"

Amy stood. "Let's get out of here."

"Where are we going?"

"To find your light. I'm not getting a panda vibe from you."

"You're not?"

"Nope," Amy said, stealing a glance at the slick of bacon grease on Sadie's plate. "Not seeing it."

Sadie nodded. She didn't feel like a panda. But what did she feel like? An insect? A mean hyena? She certainly wasn't a giraffe. Her grades weren't good enough for her to be a monkey. And she was too fast to be a sloth. "A panda wouldn't be so bad. It might be nice to be a cute cuddly for a change."

"Maybe," Amy said. "But cute cuddlies don't get very far around here."

"Yeah," Sadie said, standing. That much was clear. The rest, however, remained a total mystery.

four

"**D**o you crave bamboo?" Amy asked, pen hovering over her notebook as they crossed the grassy field behind Charm House.

"I'm not a panda," Sadie said. "My eyes are like this because I don't sleep."

Amy jotted down the word *nocturnal*. "The clearing is a much better place to conduct my tests. It's a half mile away, so the nosy ones with hypersensitive ears can't eavesdrop. But we should stay close because of the whole Kate thing."

Sadie nodded. She really wanted to ask why the Pack thought Amy got rid of Kate on purpose. And, more important, were they right? Because if they were, Amy was a serious meanie. And if they were wrong, shouldn't they stop blaming her?

They arrived at the edge of the property, where the school's field ended and the forest began. Where leaves rustled and gnarled roots jutted out of the ground. Where bad things happened to girls named Kate.

"Why is the Pack so mad at you?" Sadie blurted. Yes, she *wanted* to identify her animal light, assuming that was a real thing. But she *needed* to know what Lindsey and Taylor had been talking about in the Caf. Because if Amy was snaky, maybe Sadie was in danger, too. "Why do they think the Kate thing was your fault?"

Amy gazed into the distance and sighed, floating the black wisps of hair that escaped from her topknot skyward. Once the strands settled around her pale face, she fixed her gaze on Sadie, as if trying to determine whether the "raw meat" could be trusted.

"I'm an awesome secret keeper," Sadie assured her. "I don't have friends, so who would I tell?"

The corners of Amy's mouth lifted, changing her expression into something resembling relief. The teapot was finally ready to spill. "Long story longer, Lindsey has always been the queen of the jungle around here—"

"Yeah," Sadie said, "she made that clear during breakfast."

"Then, last year, Val, Mia, and Liv showed up—"

"Hyenas?"

Amy nodded. "And they wanted to take over. They kept trying to turn people against Lindsey, but it never worked, so one night they ganged up on her in the Watering Hole and challenged her to a fight."

"Like, a real one?"

"No, a dance-off," Amy said. Then, "Of course a real one,

which is against Charm House rules. We're taught to control our instincts so our instincts don't control us. And those girls were out of control. Anyway, right when the hyenas were about to pounce, Kate showed up and the two cats scared them off. That's when Lindsey and Kate realized that together they were unstoppable."

"Then what?" Sadie asked, anxious for her to get to the part about Kate being sent away. The reason why Amy had stopped at the edge of the woods and didn't dare go deeper.

"Long story medium, Kate brought me in because I was her roommate and best friend, and Lindsey brought in Taylor because they were roommates and best friends. Soon everyone started calling us the Pack."

"Okaaaay," Sadie said, her patience thinning like the morning mist.

"Anyway, Kate and I always joked about who would be queen if Lindsey left. Kate's a cat so, technically, it should be her, but she had a fierce temper and was failing Instinct Control class, whereas I am seriously patient and I'm getting straight As in IC, so . . ."

"Then what?"

"Kate and I were hanging in the clearing last weekend, debating the whole queen thing, and she roared a little too loud and . . ."

"And *what*?"

"Some hunters heard her. They cocked their guns and crept toward us like we were actual animals or something. I closed my eyes, curled into a tiny ball, and froze. But not Kate. She pounced on them the first chance she could. She hates hunters. We all do. But she hates them enough to hurt them. And from the sound of it, that's what she did."

Sadie's breath hitched. "How bad was it?"

"Bad, especially since one of them turned out to be Sheriff Skinner. While he cuffed Kate, his whimpering, bleeding buddy called IBS. And who knows what's happening to her now. I miss her so much." Tears began slithering down Amy's cheeks.

Sadie tried to imagine herself in that situation. Would she have attacked the hunters and tried to free her friend? Would she have run off to get help? Or would she, like Amy, have curled into a tiny fear ball?

"It's not your fault," Sadie said. "I would have been petrified."

"Yeah, well, try telling that to Lindsey and Taylor."

The thought of telling Lindsey and Taylor anything made Sadie's stomach roil.

"Wanna know the worst part?" Amy asked.

"It gets worse?"

"Now that Kate is gone, Lindsey is back to being a lone cat, and—"

"The hyenas?"

"Yep. And she said if they mess with her power, her pride, or her nails, it's *my* fault."

Sadie opened her mouth to respond, but nothing came out. What did friends say to make each other feel better?

"Anyway, moving on," Amy erased the uncomfortable thoughts with a shake of her head. "I want to test your ascension skills." She lifted her notebook and click-clicked her pen. "Climb that big-leaf maple. If you make it to the first branch with those chewed-up fingernails, it will prove you're scansorial, which is a key factor in determining your light."

Sadie made a mental note to search up the word *scansorial* when she got back to the room. Then she squinted to evaluate the tree. It had an overgrown canopy of yellowing leaves and a trunk that looked squat by comparison. Still, the first branch was at least nine feet high. Nails or no nails, was this even possible?

She approached the maple like an enemy, all the while secretly listening for the sheriff's creeping footsteps, the cock of his rifle, the scamper of a frightened deer. Then an unfamiliar scent caught her by surprise.

"Do you smell that?" she asked.

Amy lifted her nose to the air and sniff-sniffed. "It wasn't me."

Sadie giggled. "Not that kind of smell."

"Is it like cages and torture devices? Is it someone from IBS?"

Sadie shook her head. This was an inviting smell. It was sensitive and smart, friendly but serious. It was like a grape-scented eraser.

Sadie's brain told her to run back to school. But every instinct in her body urged her to find this adorable creature before it got away. And when her brain and body disagreed, her body usually won. "It's coming from the clearing."

"You can smell the clearing from here?" Amy asked, quickly making note. "Can you see it, too?"

"Is it that open space with the black trees?"

"Yeah. They were burned in last year's wildfires—"

"Follow me!" Sadie said, captivated by the delicious sweet scent.

"Wait!" Amy called after her. "It's too dangerous!"

"What if it's a purple unicorn?" Beast was in control now. And it wasn't going to stop until it identified this glorious smell.

Sadie leapt over fallen logs and knobby tree roots, oblivious to her tired, aching limbs. She felt so free, so curious, so alive!

As the grape-eraser smell intensified, Sadie slowed her pace. Heart thumping, she tiptoed across the uneven terrain, careful not to snap a twig or crush a crispy leaf for fear of alerting the mysterious being to her presence.

Then *smack!* Somewhere an open book was quickly shut.

"Who's there?" asked a boy, his cracking voice ravaged by puberty.

That's my purple unicorn?

Sadie considered hiding, but Beast wasn't the least bit afraid. It told her to risk everything and get closer. Besides, if the boy *was* dangerous, he wouldn't smell like a grape-scented eraser. He'd smell like a regular eraser that had been soaked in cat pee, the way most dangerous people smell.

"I said, who's there?" he cracked.

"It's me," Sadie said, inching toward his voice, that smell. She found him sitting under a cedar tree holding something behind his back. His eyes a distracting shade of grass green, his hair spiky and dark except for the sun-bleached tips. Sadie thought of the snowcapped peaks on Mount Rainier. How she loved to stare at those mountains . . .

She quickly pulled up the hood of her sweatshirt, concerned more with her hair than with her safety.

"Who are *you*?" he asked.

"You tell me first."

"Brett," he said. "But everyone calls me Beak."

"Because of your nose?"

His hand went to the arching slope of his nasal bone. He chuckled. "No, because my last name is Van der Beak."

Sadie's cheeks warmed. "Sorry."

Why had she said that? Why couldn't she control herself? She glanced back toward Charm House, desperate for Amy to arrive and make things less awkward. No such luck.

"So, um, what are you hiding behind your back?" She also wanted to know why Beak was alone in the woods and where he'd gotten the C-shaped scar on his cheek. But if he was hiding a hatchet or, say, a decapitated head, who cared where he got that scar.

"What am I hiding? What are *you* hiding?"

"What do you mean?"

He indicated the hood tied tightly around her face.

"I got it from the sale bin at my mother's yoga studio," she said, answering the question she wished he had asked instead.

"There you are!" Amy was huffing as she approached the clearing, notebook stuffed in the waistband of her flannel pajama bottoms. "Your incredible speed indicates that—" She stiffened at the sight of Beak. "*This* is the purple unicorn?"

Beak's eyebrows shot up. "Purple unicorn?"

"Let's go, Zendaya," Amy said. "We need to get back to our picnic." Without another word, she wrapped her frigid hand around Sadie's wrist and tugged.

"Zendaya?" Sadie giggled. "And what picnic—?"

Amy tugged even harder. "Bye, stranger in the woods! Nice meeting you." She was walking quickly now, almost running.

"Wait! Amy, what's happening right now?"

"Shhh," Amy hissed as she dragged Sadie along. *"Stop talking!"*

Once they were out of the clearing and back on the lush green lawn of Charm House, Amy let go of Sadie's wrist. "I called you Zendaya because I didn't want him to know your real name."

"But *Zendaya?*"

"Why not?" Amy smiled, revealing her fangs. "She's perfection."

"Does that mean you think I'm perfection?" Sadie asked, mostly joking but a little bit serious.

"It means you never should have talked to him."

"Why, do you think he works for IBS?"

"What? No!" Amy laughed as if that were the most ridiculous question Sadie could possibly have asked—a little unfair, considering that everything about the past two days had been ridiculous.

"Then what?"

"He probably goes to Allendale, the private boys' school down the road."

"Do the boys have animals living inside them, too?" Sadie thought of Beak's nose, his nickname. He was probably a bird.

"No one knows, so we have to be careful. If they are Typicals and they discover what we are, they could report us. Then all of this"—she indicated the majestic trees, the acres of bright green foliage—"would be gone. Correction: All of this would still be here. We would be gone." Amy shook her head. "God, Sadie, what were you thinking?"

Sadie hadn't been thinking; she'd been *feeling*. And the feeling she got when she thought of Beak's mountain-peak hair, his berry-colored lips, and that C-shaped scar was sparkly. It made her insides feel bubbly and animated, like the mist that dances over a freshly poured soda. "I guess I was thinking he's cute."

Amy giggled. "He is, actually." Then, more seriously, "Now forget you ever saw him. Okay?"

"Okay," Sadie lied. Because how was she supposed to do that?

That night as Sadie tossed and turned in bed, she wasn't thinking about snoring or sleeplessness. She wasn't even wondering whether Amy could be trusted or what horrors Kate might be enduring. Her sole focus was on the jittery feeling inside her belly. Was it the animal living inside her? Or was it love? The possibility of either one being real was disconcerting. The possibility of both being real was next-level unfathomable. And yet that effervescent mist was still dancing inside her, and it showed no signs of stopping anytime soon.

five

*A*t five o'clock Monday morning, under the charcoal-colored darkness of a predawn sky, thirty-two silent girls walked single file across the misty Charm House lawn. Each one was shrouded in a black velvet cloak embossed with an image of her animal light on the back.

Miss Flora was leading the procession and had placed Sadie directly behind her. She promised Sadie's cloak would come after the ceremony, once they'd determined what was living inside her. Until then, she would have to wear the school uniform—a safari-beige jumpsuit that unfortunately did not come with a hair-hiding hood.

How Miss Flora was going to determine Sadie's light remained a mystery—one that Amy refused to help her solve.

"It will ruin the surprise," she said when Sadie woke her up and begged her to spill.

"That's the point. I don't want to be surprised. And why does everyone have to watch?"

"What are you so afraid of?"

"Nicknames," Sadie said, anticipating the teasing she'd have to endure once her light had been identified. What would it be this time: Bark Simpson? Rat Damon? Lamb I Am?

"I hear ya," Amy said. "Everyone at my old school called me Fangzilla."

"They called me Hairy Poppins."

Amy giggled. "Your bullies were more creative than mine."

"Lucky me."

Miss Flora stopped in front of an old barn at the edge of the property, pausing to sort through an iron ring of keys. When she found the right one, she simply pressed it against the splintering wood and stood back. The door creaked open: no keyhole, no unlocking, no clue how it worked.

The inside smelled like dried oats and earth, exactly the way Sadie had expected it would. It was the circle of hay bales around the barn's perimeter and the antique carousel at its center that Sadie had not expected.

With a warm hand on Sadie's shoulder, Miss Flora gently but firmly moved her aside so the other girls could enter. As they passed, Sadie listened for catty comments. Did they resent her because they had to wake up so early? Were they planning to humiliate her? Was someone making fun of her hair? But she didn't detect a single sound.

Once everyone was seated, Miss Flora guided Sadie to the throne by the carousel's center pole. Sadie's heart quickened.

Beast stirred. The dried-oats-and-earth smell was replaced with the acetic tang of vinegar. It was fear. Her own.

"All rise and remove your hoods for the benediction," Miss Flora said.

Sadie stood.

A few girls giggled.

"Not you," Miss Flora said. "You stay seated."

"Sorry," Sadie muttered as thirty-two girls in black velvet cloaks began to recite:

> *It is with humble gratitude we invite*
> *The deity who gave us our might.*
> *A new light is here, thanks to thee.*
> *Please reveal who she might be.*

The girls lifted their hoods, sat back down, and began chanting, *Clip, snip, prick . . . Clip, snip, prick . . . Clip, snip, prick . . . Clip, snip, prick . . .*

"Nurse Walker, please step up to the throne," Miss Flora said.

Clip, snip, prick . . . Clip, snip, prick . . . Clip, snip, prick . . .

A woman with wild red curls and safari-beige scrubs approached Sadie. There was a silver tray balanced in her open palm. She smelled like the ear-piercing pagoda at Cloverfield Mall—antiseptic, with the promise of pain.

Clip, snip, prick . . . Clip, snip, prick . . . Clip, snip, prick . . .

Sadie's heart was beating so hard that she could feel it thumping in her scalp. She began nibbling her thumbnail. What if Miss Flora was a nefarious research scientist? What if these black-cloaked girls were under her hypnotic spell? What if this wasn't a "safe place" called Charm House after all? What if this was IBS?

Clip, snip, prick . . . Clip, snip, prick . . . Clip, snip, prick . . .

Sadie sprang to her feet. "I'm outta here!"

Without a word, Miss Flora rested that warm hand of hers on Sadie's shoulder and guided her back into her seat. The headmistress's touch wasn't forceful or firm. It was reassuring—a silent promise that everything was going to be fine.

"I'm Nurse Walker," said the wild-haired woman. "And this isn't going to hurt one bit."

"That's what nurses always say right before they do something that hurts," Sadie said.

The girls giggled again. At her or with her, she didn't know.

"First I'm going to clip a tiny piece of your fingernail," Nurse Walker said. "If I can find one you haven't chewed on . . ."

Clip, snip, prick . . . Clip, snip, prick . . . Clip, snip, prick . . .

Sadie shot Amy a wide-eyed look of desperation. *Help me!*

Amy flashed an encouraging thumbs-up from the crowd. *You've got this!*

Clip, snip, prick . . . Clip, snip, prick . . . Clip, snip, prick . . .

After a painless clip of her pinky nail, Nurse Walker said, "Snip," as she cut a strand of Sadie's hair. Then, before Sadie could stop her, she poked her fingertip and drew a spot of blood. "All done!" She placed the samples into a copper bowl, handed it to Miss Flora, and disinfected Sadie's fingertip before bandaging it.

Finally, the chanting stopped.

"Now for the fun part," Miss Flora said. She placed the copper bowl in a hatch at the base of the carousel. "Behold . . ."

An engine whirred. The bulb lights popped on. Organ music played. The platform spun. Hydraulic brass rods began lifting and lowering the wooden animals.

As the gears picked up speed, giraffes, snakes, owls, monkeys, lions, tigers, eagles, lizards, hyenas, chameleons, leopards, jaguars, rats, cats, and dingoes whipped by in a dizzying blur.

The girls in the audience started rooting for their favorites. But unlike the others, Sadie didn't want answers. There was comfort in not knowing; good news was still possible. But once the truth was out, she would be forced to own it, live it, and be nicknamed it—and all hope for something better would be gone.

What was *something better, though?* Sadie wondered. *What do I even want to be?* She had spent so long fixating on the traits she *didn't* want, she never stopped to consider the ones she *did*.

Minutes later, the whirring slowed, and one by one the animals locked into place. First the lizards, then the giraffes, then the wolves, the monkeys, the dingoes, the owls, the tigers, the eagles, the snakes . . . until only three types remained. The rats settled next. Then the hyenas.

The music faded. The lights dimmed. The platform slowed to a stop. And yet one pair of animals continued to rise. They had their answer, and everyone began hissing with delight.

"Yes!" Amy shouted. "I knew it!"

Lindsey and Taylor gasped.

The hyenas exchanged looks of concern.

Sadie was stunned.

"A lion!" Miss Flora beamed. "Finally." She stopped one of the wooden animals and removed a black velvet cloak from its saddle. "We've been waiting for you."

The hisses got louder.

It was the perfect time for a gracious tip of the head and a humble hand to the heart. But Sadie couldn't muster either of those reactions. She didn't give herself lion light, how could she take credit for it? And why had they been waiting for her? What did they need Sadie to do? What did all this mean?

She cut a look to Amy and instantly envied her enthusiasm. She was hissing and waving her arms in the air. She knew exactly what this meant.

Sadie grimaced. "What?" she mouthed.

"No more nicknames," Amy whispered, knowing Sadie could hear her. "You're a leader now." She flashed a proud fangy smile. "Welcome to the jungle."

Sadie finally tipped her head. But it wasn't gratitude she was feeling. It was stone-cold fear.

six

Sadie hurried to claim the desk next to Amy's, only to realize that hurrying to claim anything was no longer necessary. She was a lion. Boss lady of the food chain. The girl Charm House had been waiting for. No one dared whisper about her during breakfast for fear of her overhearing. They averted their eyes as a sign of respect and stepped aside to let her pass.

Sadie smiled at her classmates, hoping to convey that she was still the same kind, humble, insecure mess she had been three hours earlier—before the status upgrade. But no one looked her way long enough to notice. Except for Lindsey. When their eyes met, a slow grin spread across the tigress's face like she had just been served a meal she couldn't wait to devour. And Sadie had a chilling sense that *she* was that meal.

"We need to jump-start your jumpsuit," Amy said just as the first-period gong sounded.

"We need to *what*?"

Before Amy could answer, Professor Jo entered the room,

and Sadie forgot all about, well, everything. Unlike the teachers at Timor Lake Middle, with their approachable haircuts, sensible sneakers, and practical wardrobes, this woman was one tour bus away from being a full-blown rock star. Her short platinum-blond hair was a mess of choppy layers; smudges of kohl lined her hazel eyes; and her nose—a strong curve that made Sadie think of Beak—held a glinting diamond stud. And there was nothing practical about the black feathers hanging off the sleeves of her jumpsuit, or her worn combat boots with yellow laces. It didn't matter what subject Professor Jo was about to teach: Sadie was all ears.

"Why is everyone so quiet this morning?" she said, with the amused grin of someone who knew exactly why. "Is it because we have a majestic creature in our presence?"

Prickles of heat bloomed across Sadie's body. If her classmates hadn't noticed her already, they certainly did now.

"Welcome to Instinct Control, Sadie," Professor Jo said, eyes fixed and searing. "We're happy to have you." Then, to the others, "Aren't we, ladies?"

Everyone hissed, a much less intimidating sound now that the black cloaks were off. But the intimidation was far from over. Like Professor Jo, each girl wore a personalized jumpsuit. There were pins, scarves, sequins, paint splotches, patches, fringes, pompoms, and doodles—anything and everything to set them apart from the herd. While Sadie's uniform was still out-of-the-bag basic—no flavor, no pizzazz, no taste. Plain as her mother's sugar-free yogurt. Is that what Amy had meant about jump-starting her jumpsuit? Because, seriously? Along with making friends, finding her classes, understanding her powers, and crushing on a boy she might never see again, was Sadie supposed to worry about fashion, too? Oh, and what about her schedule? She peered down at the paper she'd received from Miss Flora after the ceremony. Were these subjects even real?

FIRST PERIOD: *Instinct Control—Cave #301*
SECOND PERIOD: *Speed and Stamina—Back Lawn*
THIRD PERIOD: *Cat Health and Hygiene—Shade #104*
FOURTH PERIOD: *Scent Identification—Shade #102*
FIFTH PERIOD: *Typical Topics—Shade #100*
 (Learn what Typicals study in public schools so you don't fall behind.)
SIXTH PERIOD: *Leadership for Lions—Den*

"Before you got here, I bet you felt like you had a wild beast living inside you," Professor Jo said, not like a teacher, but like someone who understood.

Sadie nodded at what had to be the biggest understatement of the century.

"And I bet it's a relief to know your true identity."

Sadie nodded again because, yes, there was tremendous relief in knowing. Her hair wasn't unruly; it was a mane. She didn't have insomnia; she was nocturnal. Her exhaustion wasn't a cry for attention; it was a cry for a catnap. Her keen eyesight, her sensitive sense of smell, her speed . . . there was an explanation for all of them.

"But knowing what is inside you is only half the battle," Professor Jo explained. "The other half is . . ."

"Knowing how to tame it," the girls answered together.

"And that's where I come in. My class will teach you how to control your natural instincts so you can live in the real world without being . . ."

"Detected," the girls said.

Pleased, Professor Jo perched on the corner of her desk and smiled at her flock. "Sadie, would you mind grabbing a ream of paper off the supply shelf?"

Chairs creaked as several girls shifted forward in anticipation of whatever was about to happen next.

"Uh, okay," Sadie said, unclear as to why Professor Jo couldn't do it herself. The shelf was to the left of her desk, while Sadie was seated in the back of the classroom. But she did what she was told and grabbed the thick brick, then deposited it on the teacher's desk. It landed with a dense *thunk*.

"Perfect," Professor Jo said. "I need to cut these in half so I'll just—" She ripped through the ream with her bare hands as if it were a single sheet of paper and not a stack of five hundred.

The girls giggled. They must have seen this trick before. But Sadie was so shocked that she let out a non-leonine squeak.

"On second thought," Professor Jo added as she unlaced her boots, "I need these sheets cut into quarters." With that, she kicked off her combats, pulled off her socks, and tore the even thicker stack apart with her bare feet.

Sadie's hand flew to her open mouth. "How did you—"

"Eagle light," she said as she slipped back into her boots. "I can break a man's wrist with my hands. I can spot a rabbit from a mile away. And while I can't fly, I can jump twenty feet in the air. But I don't. I use paper cutters, binoculars, and ladders. I've trained myself to do things like a Typical, and I'm going to train you, too. Sound like a plan?"

Sadie nodded. *Typical* sounded nice for a change.

"As you all know, Kate was picked up by the Institute of Behavioral Science last week." She dabbed at the corners of her eyes with the feathery sleeve of her jumpsuit. "It's a tragedy that could have been prevented had I only . . ." She dabbed again.

"It's not your fault," Amy muttered.

"Agreed," Lindsey said, sharpening her nails with that gold file of hers. "It's yours," she said to Amy.

"Miss Striker!" Professor Jo snapped.

"It's also society's fault," Lindsey added. "For expecting us to deny our true natures."

"Yes. But since we can't change society, we have to change . . ."

"Ourselves," the girls responded.

"Exactly. And I've come up with a practical way to apply that work."

Sondra, a petite rat light, sighed. "Does that mean more tests?"

"Yay, tests!" Rachel, a monkey light, clapped. She was bouncing in her chair, restless and joyful.

Several girls groaned.

"Wait! Listen to what I have in mind before you start complaining. It's risky, but it involves real-world experience that I think you'll all appreciate."

"Does that mean we're finally getting out of here?" Lindsey asked.

"No, Lindsey. It means I've found a practical way for you to practice self-control."

"Why do we have to control ourselves?"

Taylor sighed. "Here we go again."

"We should be taught to celebrate our instincts," Lindsey pressed. "Not to cover them up like a bunch of chin zits. No offense, Sondra."

"Tons taken," the rat snipped, then concealed her pimply skin behind a wall of oily beige hair.

"If anyone needs to control their instincts, it's the Typicals. They're the ones who discriminate. They should be the ones changing, not us."

"I understand why you feel that way, Lindsey. I know how hard it is to be sent away and forced into hiding because you don't fit in with other people's ideas of normal. But the world is a dangerous place for lights, and accepting that fact instead of resenting it is the only way to stay safe." She began to pace in front of the whiteboard. "You have all been blessed with amazing gifts. While we want you to get the most out of them, we also need you to learn to control them. We want you to be yourselves. Just not all the time."

"But—" Lindsey began.

Professor Jo silenced Lindsey with a flash of her palm. "I'm not suggesting more tests. I'm suggesting a dance."

The girls exchanged glances.

"A dance?" Lindsey asked, rolling back her shoulders. "Who with?"

"The Allendale boys."

The glances quickly became hisses of approval. Though no one was more excited than Sadie. There was a part of her that had been wondering if she'd ever see Beak again.

"It's risky," Professor Jo said. "The goal is to stay in control no matter what the boys do, or you will be discovered. *We* will be discovered. But it's a step toward testing you in the real world, and with a few weeks of intensive training, you should be ready."

Lindsey's hand shot up. Gold bangles clanged as they slid toward her elbow. "Can Taylor and I run the planning committee?"

Professor Jo smiled, as if she had expected nothing less. "Does anyone object?"

No one dared.

"Very well. Let's schedule a time to meet, and we can go over the details."

"Me-ow!" Taylor said.

Does she know she isn't a cat?

Several girls leaned toward them, whispering congratulations and requesting to join the committee, but Lindsey swatted them away like flies.

When the gong sounded, Sadie gathered her things and followed Amy toward the door. So what if she was a mighty lion? She felt mousy and planned on sticking to Amy like a flea in fur. "What class do you have now?"

"Serpent Strategies," Amy said. "But I have to swing by Miss Flora's office first for a venom drain."

Sadie looked up from her schedule. "Huh?" She had a vague recollection of Amy talking about her venom over breakfast, but post–Charm Ceremony shock combined with first-day-of-school jitters had a way of making a girl forget.

"My body produces too much venom, which can be toxic, so I drain it and give it to Miss Flora." They stepped into the dimly lit hall and joined the midmorning bustle. "Hey, I have an idea . . . ," Amy announced, as if it had just come to her. "You should use your status to get us into the Pack. Like, demand it, or something."

"Seriously?" Sadie drew back her head. "Even if I could, which I can't, why would you want that? Those girls are super mean to you."

Sadie instantly wished she could take her words back. Not because Amy looked gutted by her honesty—which she did—but because those preachy sentiments made Sadie sound like a grown-up lecturing a kid on self-esteem, and those lectures never helped. Yes, it was twisted to kiss the butts of your bullies, but anyone who had ever had her spirits flat-ironed by a mean girl knew that the best way to avoid being hunted was to befriend the hunter. Or, at the very least, to be the sidekick who gives her a Perrier after an exhausting kill.

"They're only mean because of the whole Kate thing, and I need them to know I'm innocent. They were my family here. Now I don't have anyone."

What about me? Sadie wanted to shout. *You have me!* But their conversation was interrupted by Lindsey and Taylor, who wedged themselves in and bumped Amy aside.

"Hey, Sadie Lady," Lindsey purred. "Congrats on your cat stat."

"My what?"

"Cat status," Taylor clarified. "It's a pretty big deal."

"It's not *that* big a deal," yipped Val, the shortest of the three hyena lights.

"Neither are you," Lindsey said as she wrapped her arm around Sadie's shoulders and gave her a territorial squeeze.

"Me-ow," Taylor said. "Good one!" Sadie bit down on her thumbnail.

"Ew," Lindsey said. "Your hands! We need to deal with those chewed-up nails of yours. A cat needs her claws, *ma chérie,* and your fingers look like nubby baby carrots. Anyway, we have plenty of time for that. First, we need to talk about the dance."

"The dance? What about it?"

"Lindsey, maybe you should wait until we're alone," Taylor said, hate-glaring Amy.

"Uh, that's okay," Amy said, her eyes wide and pleading. *Make them forgive me. Get me back in the Pack* they seemed to say.

Sadie wide-eyed her back. *I'll try.*

Satisfied, Amy waved goodbye and said, "See you at lunch."

Once Amy was out of earshot, Lindsey said, "She's wrong

about that. You're hanging with us. We need a third for the dance committee, and we choose . . . *you*."

Sadie's stomach lurched. Not only had she just made plans with Amy, she did not appreciate being used to ward off hyenas. And what was a dance planning committee? But Lindsey was looking at her with those hypnotic green eyes, eyes that promised her safety, companionship, and a middle school experience that wasn't miserable.

"Lunch sounds purrfect," Sadie said, just like Lindsey would have. If she could convince them to let Amy back in the Pack, maybe, just maybe, Amy would forgive her the lunch ditch. But what if she couldn't?

seven

"**H**ere's the plan," Lindsey said, stopping short of the Caf doors. "Bag something easy, like a sandwich or a hot dog, and let's meet back here in five."

"Seriously?" Taylor blink-blinked. "For one thing, a hot dog *is* a sandwich—"

"Um, hello, a hot dog is *not* a sandwich."

"Um, hi, yes, it is. Two slices of bread with meat in the middle is a sandwich."

"Um, hey, a bun isn't two slices," Lindsey insisted. "It's a single loaf."

"Um, how's it going, a single loaf is not food. It's what Ali Crawford forgot to flush this morning." Taylor dropped an invisible microphone and kicked it down the hall.

The girls laughed themselves teary while Sadie just stood there, waiting awkwardly for them to stop. No wonder Amy missed being part of the Pack. Lindsey and Taylor had created a world built on inside jokes and playful banter. A world where they could poke fun at one another with love, the way sisters might. A world that wrapped them in soft, doughy goodness and sheltered them from pain—a hot dog bun of happiness.

"Idea!" Taylor said. "Let's skip the whole bagging thing and eat in the Caf."

Lindsey's smile faded fast. "Ew, why?"

"Whoever took Kate could still be out there."

"Honestly, Tay. When did you become such a chamele-yawn?"

Taylor's skin turned the same granite gray as the wall behind her. "What are you implying?"

"I'm not implying anything. I'm flat-out saying you've lost your sense of adventure."

"Lost it?" Taylor snorted. "When did I have it?"

Lindsey tap-tapped her chin. "Hmmmm. You were definitely more fun a few weeks ago."

"That was *before*."

"Before what?"

"Before Kate was taken, before the hyena lights started circling, before—"

"Ew, ew, and ew." Lindsey's upper lip curled in disgust. "This whole 'I'm afraid' thing of yours is starting to feel like wet wool pajamas."

Taylor cocked her head. "Wet wool pajamas? What does that even mean?"

"It means your obsession with playing it safe is making me feel itchy, irritated, and ready for bed."

"Well, your obsession with *not* playing it safe is going to get us sent to the Thirteenth Floor."

"Charm House *is* no different from the Thirteenth Floor. We're trapped either way, and I'm over it." She turned to Sadie. "Eating outside would feel much more liberating, don'tcha think?"

Sadie agreed. Not because she loved nature or wanted to feel liberated, but because she didn't want Amy to see her with Lindsey and Taylor. Sure, Sadie could say that ditching was part of her plan to get Amy back in the Pack. And Amy would probably believe her. But it wouldn't be true. The truth was, girls like Lindsey and Taylor never asked girls like Sadie to join them for lunch. And when they did, girls like Sadie ditched their real friends and said yes.

After bagging their chosen meals, Lindsey led the way to the tree houses in the oaks behind the school. They were hard to spot at first because their walls were covered in leaves, not fun shades of pink and purple; not zigzags or stripes or polka dots or hearts, as Sadie would have expected. Like the girls of Charm House, their job was to blend in, not to stand out.

"What are those used for?"

"They were built for the monkey lights," Taylor explained. "They wanted to study in the trees, and Miss Flora wanted them inside regular classrooms, so she built those to help them transition. It was such a success that the monkey lights don't even use them anymore. Now they prefer to stay indoors."

"Geeks," Lindsey muttered.

"More like *eeps,*" Sadie said, making a monkey sound.

Lindsey laughed, but Taylor couldn't even bring herself to smile. She was too busy scanning the trees for threats.

"That's the one!" Lindsey said, pointing at the oak on the far left. "It has beanbags and a cross breeze. Come on, let's climb!"

Sadie searched the trunk for a ladder but these tree houses were designed with a different kind of climber in mind—the kind who didn't need help getting up.

Lindsey took a running start, leapt onto the trunk, and was up the tree after three effortless hops. Her hands and feet didn't struggle to get a hold; her muscles didn't shake under the strain of her weight. She was pure, gravity-defying power. No wonder she didn't want to hide behind the iron gates of Charm House. Her strength was something to behold. To envy. To make her TikTok-famous.

Taylor's approach was more methodical. Instead of shooting straight up, she corkscrewed to the top. "Your turn!" she called.

Sadie approached the oak and wrapped her arms around its trunk. *Now what?* She hoped her magic would kick in the way Harry Potter's did when he ran full throttle into that wall at the train station. If he could slip through bricks unscathed, surely Sadie could climb a tree.

Only she couldn't.

With her arms wrapped around the bumpy bark, Sadie tried to focus on the sensation of "up-ness," but her magic failed to appear.

"Dig your nubby baby-carrot fingers into the tree and climb," Lindsey called.

Sadie lifted her leg, hugged the trunk with her inner thigh, and dug her baby carrots in deep. Still . . . nothing.

"Is she peeing?" Taylor asked.

Lindsey giggled. "She looks like a dog light."

Sadie lowered her leg. "I—I don't know how to do this!"

"Take a running start!"

"Leap!"

"Engage your core!"

"Trust your muscles!"

Sadie tried it all. After ten unsuccessful minutes, she collapsed onto the ground. How was she supposed to trust her muscles if they kept betraying her?

"We'll work on it," Lindsey said.

As she and Taylor scampered down the trunk, Sadie gazed up at the tree branches that made puzzle pieces of the sky and wished they had never invited her. *Lindsey was probably hoping for a fierce predator to help her ward off the hyenas. Not some stubby-nailed tree humper.*

"No one gets to the top on their first try," Lindsey said, as if reading Sadie's mind. "The climb takes time."

"How long did it take you?"

"About twenty seconds. But don't compare yourself to me—you'll really bum out."

"Well," Taylor said, trying her best to sound disappointed, "I guess we should probably head back."

Lindsey joined Sadie on the ground and unpacked her lunch. "*After* we eat, chamele-yawn."

"Catty much?" Taylor sat with a defeated sigh.

"Much as I can be."

"My dad and I were going to build a tree house last weekend," Sadie said, trying to distract the girls and keep them from fighting. It worked with her parents, so why not? "It was going to have Wi-Fi, furniture, and a stocked fridge. And steps. Definitely steps."

"What happened?" Taylor asked. "Why didn't you build it?"

"I ended up here."

Lindsey took a hungry bite of her extra-rare cheeseburger, and meaty juice dripped down her wrist. It mingled with her gold bangles and left pink tracks along her arm, but it didn't look gross at all. Somehow she made it look delicious. Not even Harry Potter had that kind of magic. She chewed. "I don't remember my parents. I don't remember anything about my life before Charm House. Miss Flora found me lying unconscious by the front gates two years ago. No note. No identification. No nothing."

Sadie folded a piece of bacon into her mouth. "Did anyone call the police?"

"No way!" Taylor insisted. "We have to keep this place a secret, remember?"

"So, that's . . . it?"

"Miss Flora gives me this special medicine that's supposed to help me remember, but it hasn't worked yet."

"I think I saw it in her office," Sadie said, recalling the vials of amber-colored liquid, how the labels read *L.S. Elixir.* "What does the *L.S.* stand for?"

"Dunno."

"I always thought it stood for Lindsey Striker," Taylor said. "You know, *your name.*"

"Oh yeah!" Lindsey giggled in a way that made her seem younger, more carefree than usual. Like for that one moment she wasn't a cunning tigress or the queen of a pack; she was a normal girl who made normal mistakes. But it didn't last long. She folded the last bite of burger into her mouth, then turned to face the woods and roared.

Taylor's skin turned leaf-green. "What are you *doing*?"

"Trying to get Link's attention."

"By roaring? Are you nuts?"

"It's our new mating call."

"Does he know you're a—"

"Tiger light? Why would he ever think that?"

Taylor rolled her eyes. "Well, what *does* he think when you roar?"

"That I'm good at imitating tigers."

"Who's Link?" Sadie interrupted, distracting them again.

"Lincoln Everly, the cutest boy at Allendale." Lindsey beamed. "And my date for the dance."

Taylor's beady eyes blink-blinked. "How does he know about the dance? We just found out about it this morning."

"He doesn't know *yet*," Lindsey said. "That's why I'm calling. So I can tell him."

"Maybe we should figure out the details first," Taylor suggested. "You know, make it official."

The hyenas began yipping in the distance. "You're right. We *should* make everything official." Lindsey took Sadie's hand and examined her fingers. "Let's start with these nails. They're not ready for a stripe. They need work."

"I was talking about making the dance official," Taylor muttered, "but okay."

"Stripe? What stripe?"

Lindsey and Taylor flashed their nails, showing the black stripes painted down their centers.

"Members of the Pack get a stripe," Lindsey said. "It's our mark."

Sadie looked from Lindsey to Taylor, then back to Lindsey, assuming they were messing with her. But Lindsey's emerald eyes radiated sincerity, and Taylor's leaf-green skin was returning to normal.

"You want *me* in the Pack?"

"We cats have to stay together."

"Um, I'm right here," Taylor said.

"CATCOR," Lindsey said. Then to Sadie, "It stands for Chameleons Are the Cats of Reptiles." In a whisper that was meant to be heard, she added, "Taylor needs constant reassurance."

"What about snakes?" Sadie tried. "I hear they're a cat's best friend."

"Ask Kate about that," Taylor said. "Oh, wait, you can't. She's not here . . . because of a *snake*!"

Sadie wanted to remind them that Kate had been caught because she couldn't control her instincts. That the hunters, not Amy, had turned her in. That Sadie resented being used to ward off hyenas. And that she refused to wear their stripe unless Amy could wear it, too. But instinct told her to focus on surviving, so she didn't say any of those things.

"From now on, it's paws and claws only." Lindsey declared.

And that was the end of that.

eight

When the sixth-period gong rang, everyone scattered, leaving Sadie alone in the corridor to scrutinize her schedule yet again, because all it said was:

SIXTH PERIOD: *Leadership for Lions—Den*

No floor name, no room number, no nothing. Just: *Den.*
She asked around, but not a single girl had heard of it. And while going to Miss Flora would have been the sensible thing to do, sneaking off to her room for a catnap felt better than sensible. After what was shaping up to be the most exhausting day of Sadie's life, it felt next-level *right.*

As she hurried toward the stairwell, Sadie heard the squishy squeak of Croc shoes behind her.

"Is something wrong, Miss Samson?" Ms. Finkle asked, her voice knowing and stern.

Wrong? Sadie scoffed at the understatement. Should she

remind the woman that her day had begun with a freakishly intimidating ceremony? That she just found out she was part lion instead of full human? That her classmates had decided she was too intimidating to speak to? That she had witnessed an eagle light shred a ream of paper with her feet? That she had broken lunch plans with Amy to hang with the Pack? That she had been invited to join the Pack and Amy hadn't? That she kept nodding off in her classes and couldn't recall a single thing she had learned? And that now she was expected to find a classroom that didn't seem to exist? But Sadie didn't dare say any of those things. Not when Ms. Finkle's wide amber eyes were glaring at her like that. Instead, she offered her crumpled schedule to the woman and said, "I don't know where the Den is. No one does."

Ms. Finkle handed the schedule back. "That's because you're the only student at Charm House who is allowed to use it."

"Oh." Sadie swallowed. Was she supposed to feel honored or terrified? "So, how do I find it?"

"Your instincts will guide you."

Sadie yawned. "Sorry," she said, covering her mouth. "Right now, my instincts are super tired."

"Understandable," Ms. Finkle cooed, her usual brand of hard-edge discipline softening into something more serene. "Get some rest."

Sadie cocked her head. "Seriously?"

"Yes."

"Is this a trick?"

Ms. Finkle lifted her chin and rolled back her shoulders. "Why would I be tricking you?"

"Why are you letting me cut sixth period?"

"I'm not. I'm encouraging you to trust your instincts. You'll find the Den when you're ready."

"How will I know when I'm ready?"

"Follow your—"

"Instincts," Sadie interrupted, finally starting to catch on. And yet the more she learned about Charm House, the less she understood.

nine

Sadie woke up from her nap to the sound of a note being slipped under her door.

Come over ASAP.*

*FYI, ASAP stands for
Allowing Sadie, Amy Prohibited.

The lack of signature did not pose a problem. The sender was obvious, and Sadie's relief was palpable. Amy had already left for an evening skin treatment at the Watering Hole and would be gone for hours. Sadie could run over to Lindsey and Taylor's room, then slip back into bed before Amy returned. Her feelings would be none the wiser.

Gia and Jasmine, both giraffe lights, were next door in the Pack's room when Sadie arrived. They were seated in beanbags, their long legs nestled into the grassy fibers of the hot-pink shag rug. Taylor was kneeling behind Gia, working her blond waves into what would eventually be two Mickey Mouse–type puff balls on top of her head. Beside them, Lindsey was sponging flecks of glitter on the tips of Jasmine's white-painted nails. It was a Pinteresting scene made even more fabulous by the zebra-print walls and yellow lamps that gave the room a golden glow.

Lindsey noticed Sadie and stopped sponging. "Sorry, Jas, but I need to reschedule."

Jasmine laughed.

Lindsey began packing up her supplies.

"Wait," Jasmine said, thick brows knit. "Are you serious?"

"Dead."

"You haven't even done my other hand."

"Same goes for you, G," Taylor said. "Sorry."

Gia's full lips parted. "But you only did one puff."

"I can come back later," Sadie suggested.

Lindsey growled. "No, stay." Then, to her customers, "There's some urgent business I have to deal with. Let's pick this up tomorrow. Same time. I'll throw in a free paraffin treatment to make up for it."

"On my *head*?" Gia said in a half-puff huff.

Lindsey stood and opened her door. "Uh, if that's where you want it, though I think it would be better on your hands."

Jas began collecting her things, mindful not to smudge the five nails that had just been painted. "This is so unprofessional," she grumbled, the smell of fashion-magazine perfume samples and resentment wafting off her skin.

"I agree," Lindsey said in a customer's-always-right sort of way. "Taylor will throw in a free treatment for split ends, won't you, Tay?"

"Uh, sure."

"Wait!" Jasmine examined the perfect tips of her rib-grazing black hair. "I have split ends?"

"Not for long." Lindsey grinned as she nudged them forward. "Thanks so much for being understanding. You two are the cat's meow." She pulled Gia and Jasmine into a tight hug and—poof!—their resentment was gone. No wonder Lindsey was the queen.

Sadie winced. "Sorry," she said, needing the giraffic girls to know she had nothing to do with their abrupt dismissal. But they pushed past her without so much as a glance. They didn't call her Hairy Poppins, they didn't make snoring sounds, and they didn't pronounce her name Say-DIE. They didn't say a single word. This was progress.

When Lindsey closed the door, Sadie asked what the "urgent business" was all about. "Does it have to do with the Allendale dance?" she asked hopefully, yearning for an excuse to tell them about Beak.

"Ew, no. That's weeks away. There are eleven other things we have to do first."

"Eleven?"

"Ten baby-carrot nubs and one head of hair. Come." She pat-patted a beanbag, a silent order for Sadie to sit. "We have work to do."

Taylor knelt behind Sadie and began coaxing her mane into side braids and Lindsey pushed back her cuticles with a metal torture device, all while a female rapper urged girls to stop loving people who didn't love them back. And the best part? The music was on the lowest volume. Ah, to be in the company of a cat. Finally, someone who understood the sensitive-ear struggle.

Once Sadie's baby-carrot nubs were even and clean, Lindsey packed up her supplies until only a single bottle of black polish remained. "Moving on."

"Dance talk?" Sadie asked. She was a girl with tea she was ready to spill. "Because there's a cute Allendale boy who—"

"Allendale?" Taylor released Sadie's braid. "Where did you meet an Allendale boy?"

"In that clearing where the burned trees are," Sadie said.

Taylor's Mohawk camouflaged with the zebra stripes on the wall. "It's against school rules to go that far off campus. What were you doing there?"

"Oh, I—"

Lindsey swiped her lips with gloss. "What's his name?"

"Beak," Sadie said as warmth, generated by the mere mention of his name, bloomed around her heart.

"Was he alone?" Taylor asked, zebra stripes now appearing on her arms.

"Yes."

Lindsey began filing her nails with that golden file of hers. "Cute?"

"Very."

"Was anyone following him?"

"No."

"Did you get his number?"

Sadie blushed at the thought. "No!"

"Does he know your name? Or that you go to Charm House?"

"No and no."

"You sure?" Taylor asked, pacing.

"Amy told him that my name was Zendaya and that we were late for a picnic."

Taylor gasped. "Amy was there, too? Are you, like, *trying* to get sent to IBS? Because that's exactly how she got rid of Kate. You know that, right?"

"I . . . uh—" What could she say to make them trust Amy again? Sadie's eyes darted around the room as if the right response were buried under the pile of clothes on the floor or the sprawl of papers on the desks. "It was my idea to explore the woods. Not Amy's. She didn't even want to go. I made her."

Lindsey stopped filing. "You think Beak and Link are friends? If they are, we can all hang out together. And if they aren't, we'll make them."

"Totally!" Sadie said a little too quickly to be cool.

"Meow-no-you-didn't!" Taylor snapped. Still covered in zebra stripes, she stood above Lindsey, hands on hips, and glared down at her with something resembling scorn. "It's like you *want* to get sent away."

Lindsey, unfazed, responded with a fake yawn.

"Call me a chamele-yawn all you want," Taylor hissed. "At least I'll never be a lab *cat*."

"True. You're more of a *fab* cat." Lindsey flicked her chin at Taylor's zebra-striped body. "Animal prints are super in this season."

Taylor giggled. "I can't help it. I'm scared, okay?"

"And I'm bored of you being scared, so prepare the room and let's get on with it."

Taylor turned off the music, drew the curtains, lit a sage-scented candle, and flicked off the lights.

"What's happening?" Sadie asked, trying not to sound nervous.

"Shhhh," Taylor said as she returned to her beanbag, her skin fading back to its original state. "No talking."

Lindsey shook her bottle of black polish, reached for

Sadie's hand, and began painting thin black lines down the center of each crescent-shaped nail. The brush felt ticklish, the way new beginnings often do.

When Lindsey was done, she and Taylor raised their hands and bent their fingers into claws. With a sharp nod, Lindsey instructed Sadie to do the same. "Repeat after me . . ."

"Okay," Sadie accidentally whispered back. They shushed her immediately, and then Lindsey began:

"I pledge my soul to the Charm House Pack."

"I pledge my soul to the Charm House Pack," Sadie repeated.

"I will be honest and true and have your back."

"I will be honest and true and have your back."

"These stripes on my nails are an eternal vow . . ."

"These stripes on my nails are an eternal vow . . ."

"To be fierce, to be loyal, to be the cat's meow."

"To be fierce, to be loyal, to be the cat's meow."

"No matter what happens, no matter the cause . . ."

"No matter what happens, no matter the cause . . ."

"I will hold my head high and my paws in claws."

"I will hold my head high and my paws in claws."

Lindsey and Taylor pressed their fingertips together and invited Sadie to join them. When she did, an electrical current zipped through her body. She was a predator now. A real top-of-the-food-chain kind of girl who had been invited into the hot dog bun of happiness. And she never wanted to live on the outside again.

Should Sadie have fought harder to include Amy? Yes. But she promised herself two things: One, that she would always be a good friend to Amy. And two, that she would hide her striped fingernails at all costs.

ten

*S*adie bicycle-kicked her sheets onto the floor and glared up at the ceiling. It didn't matter that her room was outer-space dark, that her belly was filled with protein, that the school's alphas had welcomed her into their pack, or that she'd lasted three days without Amy noticing her striped nails. Her brain was lit like the Fourth of July sky; her legs were twitching and ready to roam. Sleep was not an option.

Knowing that she was nocturnal should have alleviated some of the frustration. Sadie was a lion light; she had been born this way, after all. It wasn't her fault. But that only made her struggle feel hopeless. Because if she didn't cause it, she couldn't cure it. And if she couldn't cure it, she was stuck with it. Much like she was stuck with the sound of that waterfall.

She had first heard it the evening Amy gave her a tour of Charm House, its distant burble a reminder of the Buddha fountain outside her mother's yoga studio. Sadie wanted to find the source, but with everything being so new and over-whelming, she had forgotten about it. Yet the burble didn't want to be forgotten. It returned in the wee hours while the other girls slept, louder and louder each night, like it wanted to be found. And Sadie, now wide awake, was ready to find it.

She crept to her desk, mindful not to wake Amy, and got a Prowl Pass. Like all nocturnal lights, she had been allotted seven tickets, each one granting her after-hours access to the facilities should she have trouble sleeping.

"Every Monday, the number of Prowl Passes you receive will be reduced by one," said Professor Gwen, the cheetah light who taught Cat Health and Hygiene. "As you learn to change your circadian rhythms, you'll adapt to typical sleep patterns. Soon you won't need the passes anymore."

As if! Sadie thought as she tiptoed to the door and slowly turned the handle.

"Oh, hey!" Amy said, startled. She was in the hallway, key in hand, chocolate in the corners of her mouth.

Sadie glanced back at Amy's bed, the lump of pillows that looked like a body. "What are you doing out here? I thought you were sleeping."

"Late-night fudge craving. My mom gave me a box when school started, and I had one piece left."

"So you ate it in the hall?"

"I didn't want to wake you."

"How did you leave without me hearing you?"

Amy shrugged. "Quiet, I guess."

Taylor was right; she was a snaky one.

"Where are *you* going?"

Sadie flashed her Prowl Pass. "Can't sleep."

"I'm glad you're awake." Amy entered the room and began fumbling for the light.

"You are?"

"Yes! I've barely seen you all week. Now we can catch up—" She knocked over her bedside light. "Oops," she whispered as she picked it up. "I really need to wear my glasses." Then, with a giggle, "But I can't find them." She flicked on her heat lamp. An orange glow filled the room. Sadie balled her fists and hid her stripes.

"So . . . tell me everything. Don't leave one thing out."

"Everything?"

"Yeah." Amy sat on her bed and crossed her legs—a little girl ready for story time. "What's been going on?"

"Just busy with dance-planning stuff. You know, making playlists, talking themes. Taylor wants glow sticks. Lindsey's thinking glitter snow machine."

Amy cocked her head. "Glitter snow machine?"

"Yep," Sadie answered, wondering if such a thing even existed.

"So, uh, have you said anything about . . . you know what?"

"What?" Sadie asked, even though she knew.

"Me."

"Oh, that, right."

"It's been days. You must have said *something* to them. They must have said something to you."

Sadie bristled. It *had* been days. So why wasn't Amy asking about Sadie's first week of classes? What she did at night while everyone was sleeping? If she ever thought about Beak? Instead, all Amy seemed to care about was the Pack. "They think you set Kate up."

Were there kinder ways she could have responded? Absolutely. But Amy didn't seem to be considering Sadie's feelings, so why should Sadie consider hers?

"And you told them I didn't, right?"

Sadie opened her mouth to answer, but nothing came out.

"Sssseriously?" Amy hissed. "You think I set her up, too?"

"I don't know what to think. I wasn't there."

Silence, thick as the fog outside their window, settled between them.

"Let's just go to bed." Amy unclipped her yellow fanny pack and tossed it to the floor.

"It's not that I don't believe you—"

"It's fine," Amy said. "Whatever." She went to turn off the light and knocked it over. As she leaned forward to reach it, she slipped out of bed and landed on the floor with a thump.

Sadie rushed to her side. "You okay?" She held out her hand, offering to pull Amy up, but Amy just sat there stunned, her gray eyes fixed on something else entirely.

The black stripes!

Panic smacked. "Amy, I—" Sadie broke off. She *what?* What could she possibly say to justify her backstabbing behavior? That she had spent her whole life wanting to be accepted and now that she had been, she wanted to enjoy it? Sure, that made sense. But there was no justifying it. Not when Sadie's acceptance was so closely tied to Amy's rejection.

"Now I get it—" Amy began, but she was interrupted by a bloodcurdling shriek.

"Was that Taylor?" Sadie asked.

"You would know."

"'Scuse me?"

Amy hurried out of bed. "I said, let's go."

Taylor's screams echoed off the stone walls as a stampede of half-asleep girls ran toward her room, the giraffes with their endlessly long legs leading the charge.

When Sadie and Amy arrived, a crowd was blocking the open door.

"What's going on?" Sadie asked. The girls instantly cleared a path to let her through—a gesture that made her feel embarrassed and powerful at the same time.

She expected to find Taylor tangled in bedsheets, sweaty from a nightmare or creeped out by a spider. Instead, it was Lindsey who was out of sorts. "Look what I got . . . ," she slurred, satin sleep mask askew on her forehead. "S'weird, right?" She indicated her limp arm, where the number 13 had been carved into her skin.

"Someone did that to her while we were sleeping," Taylor said, her Mohawk a kaleidoscope of shifting patterns as she paced.

"What does it mean?" Sadie asked.

"It's a warning from IBS. Or maybe a threat. I dunno. But someone is clearly trying to tell us that we're all heading to the Thirteenth Floor unless—"

Sadie's chest felt tight. "Unless what?" she interrupted, her voice shrill with terror.

"I don't know!" Taylor cried.

"What's happening in there?" asked Liv, one of the three hyena lights who were starting to circle.

"Something's wrong with Lindsey," said Sondra, her chin dotted with zit cream.

Liv turned to Val and Mia. "Knock-knock."

"Who's there?" they answered.

"Opportunity."

"Opportunity who?"

"Opportunity is knocking. Let's answer!" she blurted, and the three of them started yipping with laughter.

"This isn't funny!" Gia rasped. "Someone needs to call Miss Flora."

"No!" insisted Sondra. "Lindsey hates authority."

"Since when are you an expert on Lindsey?" asked Jasmine, her giraffe lashes batting attitude.

"Since when are you?"

"Gia and I hang out with her all the time."

"Really?" Sondra cut a look to Gia's half puff and then to Jasmine's unfinished manicure. "Because Gia's hair and your nails tell another story."

"We're working on a new look," Gia said.

"Bottom line? All of us need to start locking our doors!" Taylor announced. "If we had, *she* never could have done this." Her finger was pointing straight at Amy.

"Me? You think I did this?"

"She couldn't have!" Sadie insisted. "We were in our room."

"All night?"

Sadie's cheeks grew hot. "Uh, pretty much, yeah."

"Pretty much, yeeeahhhh," Lindsey parroted, her voice spacey and loopy.

"Sadie!" Taylor snipped. "Was Amy in your room all night or not?"

"Was she *what*?"

Taylor folded her arms across her chest. "You're a lion light, Sadie. You can hear from over a mile away. So stop stalling and answer the question."

"I . . . uh . . ." Sadie lowered her eyes to the pink shag rug, wondering if Amy could have done this. The chocolate at the corners of her mouth proved she was in the hallway eating fudge. But could Amy have slipped inside the Pack's room and scratched the number 13 on Lindsey's arm while eating that fudge? She did stuff her bed with pillows and sneak off without Sadie's knowing it, so, yes, it was possible.

"I had nothing to do with this!" Amy insisted, her gray eyes pooling with tears. "Why would I hurt Lindsey?"

"Why would you hurt her?" Taylor put her hands on her hips, a fed-up mom about to school her kids. "A: jealousy, B: anger, C: revenge."

"How about D: none of the above?"

"How about E: all of the above except D."

Lindsey, who was lazily tracing her wound with the tip of her finger, slurred, "Th' so co'fusing, Tay."

Amy tugged Sadie's sweatshirt. "Let's get out of here."

Sadie froze, unsure of her next move. What if Amy had done it? What if she hadn't?

" 'S get'utta here." Lindsey giggled. "Sounds like *skedaddle hair*. Skedaddle hair, I wanna be bald."

"She's delirious. Get Nurse Walker!" Sadie shouted. The words felt awkward leaving her mouth, like she was speaking them with someone else's tongue. Was she really telling these girls what to do? As a few took off to get the nurse, Sadie stood awestruck—they were listening to her!

"That's right," Amy scoffed. "I forgot. You're one of them now."

Sadie felt the cold slap of shame. Amy had every reason

to be mad, but if Sadie could just explain that she wasn't choosing the Pack over her roommate, that she was choosing both, maybe she'd understand. "Amy, can we talk about it in our room?"

"Um, hello, you're not going anywhere with her," Taylor insisted.

"I'm not?"

"Un. Safe," Taylor muttered. "You're staying here with me. Paws and claws, remember?"

"Hold on!" Amy said. "Maybe Kate was trying to send us a message. You know how she loves to mark things."

"Me-ow!" Taylor hissed. "First you set her up, and now you're trying to frame her?" She began shooing Amy into the hallway. "Nice try, snake." She was about to slam the door when Nurse Walker arrived with a stretcher and whisked Lindsey away.

"Take Lindsey's bed," Taylor said once everyone had gone. "We'll deal with Amy tomorrow." With that, she slid under her covers and fell asleep as if nothing had happened, leaving Sadie exactly where she started: brain lit and legs twitching, wishing that the distant waterfall would shut up so she could hear herself think.

eleven

*A*t sunrise, Sadie slipped out of Taylor's room, then hurried back to her own, expecting to find Amy upset, furious, or both. Instead, she found Amy gone.

Feeling somewhat responsible, she sprang into action and traversed the entire school, hoping to track Amy's orange-and-clove scent, but she uncovered nothing. Front lawn: nothing. Back lawn: nothing. Tree houses: nothing. Barn: locked. There was only one place left, and after the previous night's chilling incident, it was not a place Sadie wanted to go.

She considered making a pro/con list to evaluate the risk, but the breakfast gong was thirty minutes from sounding. Time was running out. She asked herself what Lindsey, a real leader, would do, and seconds later, Sadie was crossing into the forbidden woods. Then the storm clouds rolled in, and rain descended on her like a punishment.

"Really?" she shouted at the elephant-gray sky.

Serves you right, weak lion light, it seemed to answer.

Determined, Sadie began trudging over saturated twigs and leaping across puddles. Her drenched *Nama'stay in Bed* sweatshirt grew heavy; hair clung to her cheeks like open tent flaps.

"Ay-meee!" she shouted at the skeletal trees.

Did Amy respond? It was hard to know. Leaves were rustling and raindrops were pelting, making it difficult to hear, even for Sadie. She tried sniffing, but all she got was a noseful of earth-brown- and forest-green-scented wind. She squinted, hoping to see through the bars of rain, but it was no use. The weather was winning; her lion light powers were useless. Funny how after a lifetime of wishing her weirdnesses away, Sadie would have given anything to have that weirdness work.

"Ayyy-meeee!" she called again, her muscles tense and aching. She wanted to rest, but the breakfast gong would ring in eleven minutes. That left five minutes to find Amy and six to get her to the Caf before Miss Flora noticed they were missing. She had to keep trying.

The wind suddenly shifted direction. Instead of blowing against Sadie's back, it whipped across her face, irritating her cheeks with its soggy chill and nipping her nose with the familiar scent of oranges, clove, and . . . *Amy!*

Sadie turned toward the scent and moved against the gale, sniffing and shouting, shouting and sniffing, until finally her supersenses led her to a girl who lay trembling on a pile of wet leaves. Her eyes were closed; her lips were shivering blue lines. "Amy!"

Dropping to her knees, Sadie reached for Amy's icy shoulder and gave her a slight shake. "Are you okay? Can you hear me?"

Pulse. Check her pulse, a voice inside Sadie said—though what she was supposed to check *for* remained unclear. Still, Sadie pushed back the sleeve of Amy's drenched fleece, hoping the answer would present itself. Though she encountered something else entirely: the number 13 scratched into Amy's forearm.

Heart racing and ears ringing, Sadie summoned her superhuman strength and carried Amy's cold, limp body through the woods and across the back lawn to the Charm House infirmary.

"You should be very proud," Nurse Walker said after wrapping Amy in foil like a baked potato and hooking her to an IV machine. "You saved her life."

Saved it? Sadie wondered. *Or almost ended it?* Had she not spent the night with Taylor, Amy wouldn't have been alone and none of this would have happened.

"Miss Flora is on her way. You should probably get going," the nurse warned.

Sadie's stomach dipped at the thought of leaving Amy. She looked so pale, so vulnerable and thin. "Is she going to be okay?"

"Yes. Her vitals are stable. She just needs rest." With a definitive tug, the nurse closed the ivory-colored curtains around Amy's bed. Visiting hours were over.

"What about Lindsey?" Sadie asked, taking in the empty beds. "Where is she?"

"I released her this morning. It's a good thing she got here when she did. It could have been much worse."

"Worse? How?" Sadie pressed, hungry for answers.

"Go to breakfast," Nurse Walker urged, wild red curls billowing around her face. "We'll take good care of her. Trust me."

Sadie hurried off, not sure who to trust. That uncertainty grew stronger after she tiptoed back to the infirmary and cracked open the door to spy.

"Come on," Miss Flora begged. "You can do this." She was standing above Amy, pressing glass vials against her fangs. "Please, dear, we need this venom."

Sadie backed away. If what Amy said was true—that she produced too much venom and had it drained to avoid toxic shock—wouldn't Miss Flora be happy about Amy's low supply? Wouldn't that be a good thing?

Instinct urged Sadie to storm in and demand answers. It also told her to run to her room and hide under her covers. In the end, she listened to her inner scaredy-cat—the only voice she trusted—and ran.

twelve

The knocking began before Sadie had a chance to change out of her soggy sweatshirt. Was it Ms. Finkle, wondering why Sadie was late for Instinct Control, or Miss Flora, asking why she'd been in the woods before breakfast? Either way, Sadie wasn't in the mood to answer. The past twelve hours had been physically and emotionally draining. She needed a moment to process.

"I know you're in there, Sadie Lady. I can hear your fear!"

It was Lindsey, sounding not at all like a girl who had been attacked in her sleep. "I can and *will* pick the lock if I have to!"

"Can and will," Taylor echoed.

Giggling, Sadie opened the door to find Lindsey dressed in a satin kimono and platform flip-flops, her yellow flower choker and gold nail file necklace prominently displayed. "Um, hello, why weren't you at breakfast?" she asked.

"Amy went missing."

"So?" Taylor tightened her plush pink robe.

"She had passed out in the woods with a thirteen on her arm. Just like Lindsey's. It was super scary and—"

"Ancient news," Lindsey said, her eyes deadened for effect. "Heard about it in the Caf. Probably did it to herself."

Sadie squinted, finding that theory hard to believe. "Why would she do that?"

"Attention. She wants it. I have it. The end." Lindsey pushed back her sleeve to reveal the mummy-style bandage around her arm, how it was decorated with colorful hearts and get-well wishes. "Classes are canceled, so let's make some tracks!"

"They are? Why?"

"Miss Flora called an emergency meeting because of what happened to Lindsey."

"And Amy," Sadie reminded them.

"Who did it for attention," Lindsey reminded her back. "Anyway, moving on. We're doing a spa day. My idea. Almost everyone is invited. Let's gooooo."

"Isn't the Watering Hole closed during the day?"

"Not for long." Lindsey lifted her gold nail file and winked. "Now suit up and meet us by the wading pools." She took in Sadie's disheveled appearance. "You could use it."

Sadie had used the showers in the Watering Hole several times but had never ventured past the frosted-glass door on the left.

The sign read *By Appointment Only,* and she had no clue how to get one. Or if she even wanted one. But that morning, the door was propped open by a towel, and the wafting scent of eucalyptus grabbed her like a much-needed hug. Whatever was back there, Lindsey was right: Sadie could use it.

She slipped inside and was instantly enveloped by a muggy mass of steam. Like a ghost, she crossed the stone floor and strained to take in her surroundings. There were three soaking pools—hot, mild, and cold—each one host to a blur of bodies. Despite the leafy vines that covered the walls, the girls' laughter and gossip-filled chitchat echoed throughout the spa.

"I think Kate escaped IBS and came back to seek revenge on the Pack," said Rachel, a monkey light who was bouncing from pool to pool, stirring up drama.

"Why would Kate want revenge on her best friends?" Jasmine asked.

"For sending her away."

"I get why Kate would do that to Amy. But why would she want to hurt *Lindsey*?"

"How do you know it's a *she*?" Taylor asked, teeth chattering as she forced herself into the cool pool. Lindsey, unaware of Taylor's sacrifice, floated peacefully beside her, bandaged arm raised to keep it dry.

"We're all *she*s," said Val, the hyena light.

"Maybe a *he* snuck in."

"Nah," Jada said. "The giraffe lights would have smelled him."

"The dingoes would have heard him," said Kara.

"And the hyenas would have crushed him," said Mia.

"Well, I have stronger senses than all of you, and I didn't hear a thing," Lindsey reminded them.

Taylor shivered. "The Scratcher is obviously working for IBS."

"Then it's Piper," said Rachel from the hot pool.

"Me? Why *me*?"

"You're a mole."

"I'm not a mole! I'm a giraffe light."

"Then what's that brown thing above your lip?"

Piper splashed water in Rachel's face. "Just because I *have* a mole doesn't mean I *am* a mole. That's like me calling you a bad-breath light because your voice smells like pickles. It doesn't work that way."

"Does too," Rachel splashed back.

"Enough!" Lindsey roared. The room fell silent. "Now listen up. I say we bust out of here, find whoever did this to me, and bring them to justice."

"We're not busting out of anywhere," Taylor said. "It's too dangerous. Anyway, how would we even do that?"

Lindsey fake yawned.

With that, Taylor stomped out of the cool pool and plunged into the hot one.

"I'll put a squad together," Lindsey continued, oblivious to Taylor's distress. "Everyone here has incredible tracking skills. . . . Well, everyone except Sondra—"

"I have seasonal allergies. It's not my fault."

"Yeah, and some freak scratched the number thirteen into my arm while I was sleeping, but you don't hear me wheezing about it."

"Sorry," Sondra squeaked. "How can I help?"

"I still think it was Amy," Val said. "You know, thinning the herd to make room for some fresh meat." She floated toward Lindsey, a devious grin on her face.

"Ew, a little space, please." Lindsey quickly lifted herself out of the pool and away from the edge.

"It wasn't Amy, okay?" Sadie announced, finally making herself known.

"Um, hello, where have you been?" Lindsey said, relief washing over her face. She waved Sadie closer.

Sadie hurried to Lindsey's side but instantly regretted it. Lindsey looked fit and fierce in a metallic bronze bikini. Next to her, Sadie, in a worn brown one-piece, felt like the poop emoji.

"How do you know it wasn't Amy?" Val pressed, her hand gliding back and forth along the surface of the water as if sharpening a blade.

"Because I'm the one who found her."

"Aha! Then it was you!"

"Me?"

"Yeah," Val said. "Whoever smelt it dealt it."

"Finding someone in the woods isn't the same as smelting it and dealt-ing it," Lindsey said, pulling Sadie closer. "Now get out and give us some space." When the others didn't leave, Lindsey roared, "GO!"

Now that they were alone, Sadie wanted to tell Lindsey what she'd seen in the infirmary and ask her why Miss Flora had been begging Amy for venom. Why she wasn't glad Amy's supply was low, since she made too much to begin with. But they were surrounded by skilled eavesdroppers, so the questions would have to wait.

Sadie dunked her head, inviting the icy water to wash the morning away. Instead, pictures of Amy lying lifeless in the woods flooded her memory: that molting frigid skin, those quivering blue lips. Sadie squeezed her eyes shut, trying to press the images into dust, but the tighter she squeezed, the more vivid they became—probably punishment for siding with the Pack instead of Amy. Because if Sadie . . . Amy probably would have been fine. But what about Taylor? Would the Scratcher have gotten her instead? The situation was impossible. As long as her friends were enemies, Sadie would always be letting someone down.

She popped up to the surface, alert but confused. All around her girls were splashing, laughing, and gossiping—curious about the mysterious intruder but not overly afraid.

They seemed confident in their ability to protect themselves, eager for the opportunity to unleash their powers and fight back. Meanwhile, Sadie, the ablest of them all, was clinging to the edge of the pool, afraid of everything. And then . . .

"Do you hear that?" she asked Lindsey.

"Hear what?"

"The waterfall. What is it?"

"Um, it's probably the waterfall," Lindsey said, with a toss of her tiger-striped hair. "I mean, if you can call it that. Technically, it's more of a water trickle."

"Oh," Sadie said, trying to sound blasé. But on the inside, her instincts were revved and ready to go, much like on the day she had picked up Beak's grape-eraser scent. Those instincts were onto something and refused to stop until Sadie was onto it, too. "Where is it?"

"Down the steps behind the hot pool."

"Did it just come on?"

"Dunno, why?" Lindsey ducked underwater, not bothering to wait for the answer. Which was fine. Sadie didn't have a reasonable one to offer. Rather than trying, she slipped out of the pool and moved toward the steps, wondering where her internal guidance system was taking her now.

thirteen

A pond the size of a blow-up baby pool lay shimmering at the base of the steps. It was too shallow to soak in and too bizarre to touch. For one thing, its surface was rainbow-colored, each arching hue a separate band that didn't bleed or blend with the others. And yet it was the curve of rocks that circled the pond's perimeter that really struck Sadie—the water that spilled gently over their smooth faces, clean and clear as glass. How such a tranquil stream could have beckoned her with such force was anyone's guess.

Sadie, wary of the rainbow pond and what it might do to her skin, reached for the waterfall instead. Before her fingers could register the silky coolness of the stream, the liquid transformed into grains of colorful sand, and the face of the rock slid open. Sadie gasped and considered running away. But her limbs were too petrified to move.

"Welcome to the Den," a female voice whispered from deep inside the darkness. Her tone was soothing yet authoritative, ancient and all-knowing. Creepy. As. Heck. "Come in."

"Uh . . ." Sadie considered calling for Lindsey when suddenly a fire whooshed on, lighting the cozy space with an inviting shade of warm gold.

"It's okay, lion. You're safe. Come inside and get comfortable. We have work to do."

Sadie inched closer to the opening and took in the familiar smell of burning wood. It conjured memories of camping trips with her father and winter nights spent reading with her mother. But this fire was more magical than all of those put together. Embers didn't float or pop. Her eyes didn't sting. It was perfectly contained and completely smokeless.

Sadie did what the Whisper told her to and got comfortable on a heap of pillows by the fire. "Hello?" she said, feeling kind of silly. If someone was there, wouldn't she have seen her? And if no one was there, who was she talking to?

The cave door closed.

"Hello," the Whisper said.

Sadie's heart began to speed.

"There's nothing to be afraid of," the voice said, somehow sensing her panic. "The Den is a safe space, made just for you. It is here that you will learn to become the great leader you were meant to be."

Sadie looked for classroom staples: a whiteboard, a laptop, a stack of dusty old books—anything to help the Whisper show her how to go from loser to leader. There was nothing. "How am I going to do that?"

"By listening."

That's it? Listening to a whisper might cure her insomnia, but set her up for greatness? Really?

"You know that feeling inside you—the one that made you flip the desks in your Language Arts class?"

"Beast?"

"Yes," she said. "Only it wasn't Beast. It was you. Being a good leader is learning to listen to that voice. Learning to trust it."

Sadie's brow furrowed. "So next time it tells me to flip a desk, I should do it?"

The Whisper snickered. "No. What you listened to was an impulse. A manifestation of your feeling. It's the actual feeling you want to listen to. That's where the message is."

"O-kayyy," Sadie said, though nothing about this was okay.

"What were you feeling when those girls called you Hairy Poppins?" the Whisper asked.

"Anger."

"Why?"

"I don't like being teased."

"So you flipped the desks because. . . ."

"I wanted them to stop teasing."

"That's it! That's what you need to tap into. The feeling of wanting to stop an injustice. I'm here to teach you how to identify that feeling and then use it in a smart and effective way."

"What if my feelings tell me to do bad things?"

"Then you will be a dangerous leader."

Sadie lowered her head into her hands. It was all too much. "Why can't Lindsey be the leader? She likes it, and everyone already listens to her."

"Lindsey leads by using fear, intimidation, and control. Noble leaders inspire and empower. They unite people who believe in a mutual cause, then help them achieve it. You can do that, Sadie. It's your—"

"Don't say destiny."

"I was going to say it's your choice. You don't have to become a leader if you don't want to. There are plenty of zoo-lion lights, girls who prefer to take on more passive roles. But if you want to lead—"

"I do!" Sadie said. "Maybe. I don't know. Who am I leading? Where are we going? Where do I start?"

"You start by figuring out what kind of person you are. What are your strengths? What are your weaknesses? What motivates you?"

"Then what?" Sadie asked.

"Add some personal touches to your uniform."

"Why my uniform?"

"It's kind of boring, don't you think?"

"That's it?"

The fire went out, and the Den door slid open. "For now," the Whisper said. "Oh, and, Sadie, the Den is for lion lights only. You must never speak of this sacred space to anyone."

"I won't," Sadie promised, because, honestly, who would believe her if she did?

fourteen

"*T*wo words, four syllables, and they work wonders for our health," Professor Esther said. "Any ideas?"

Lindsey raised her bandaged arm. "Mani-pedis!"

The professor, a strikingly beautiful puma light with tawny-beige hair and close-set blue eyes, padded to the whiteboard and wrote Lindsey's answer. "Any other thoughts?"

There were only two students in Cat Health and Hygiene besides Sadie and Lindsey: Sasha, a panther who, according to Lindsey, never washed her hands after using the bathroom, and Corinna, a perpetually homesick bobcat. Hence their exclusion from the Pack.

"What about family time?" Corinna said. "That's good for our health."

"She puts the *cat* in *catastrophe*," Lindsey whispered.

Sadie giggled like a mean girl, the kind she loathed, the kind she was in danger of becoming.

"Yes, Riri, family is important, but it's not the answer I'm looking for. Anyone else?"

"Riri?" Sadie whispered.

"Her parents call her that, so she asked the teachers to do it, too." Lindsey flicked her chin at Corrina's uniform, how she'd puffy-painted *Riri* on the back in bold green letters. "Tragic."

"What about comfortable clothes?" Sasha tried.

"What about a bar of soap?" Lindsey muttered.

"That's not two words, it's four," Sasha said, not recognizing the dig.

No longer interested, Lindsey went back to mashing wild berries. According to Professor Esther, the berries, when mixed with melaleuca oil, could heal her skin faster than any salve made by Typicals. And with the dance only two weeks away, Lindsey wanted results.

"The answer is meat substitutes," Professor Esther said, tired of her own game. "Meat substitutes are important because too much animal protein can lead to several diseases, such as—"

"Prof-Esther?" Lindsey interrupted.

The girls giggled at the nickname. Thankfully, the professor failed to notice.

"Yes, Lindsey?"

"I need more berries."

"I'm all out. Now can we *please* get back to—"

"What do you mean, all out?"

"I haven't been able to pick any. It's been raining for days."

Lindsey glanced at the window. "It's not raining now."

"I see that, Miss Striker, but *now* I happen to be teaching a lesson on meat substitutes."

"I'll pick them," Lindsey offered.

"Miss Flora does not want anyone leaving the grounds. With everything that's been happening around here, it's just not safe."

"Puuur-fessor, please, I would never want to leave," Lindsey said, clearly lying. "I just want some berries from out back."

"I'm sorry, Lindsey. My answer is no." Professor Esther shook her head and returned to the whiteboard. "Veggie burgers are a safe alternative to—"

"If it's safety you're worried about, then I *have* to go."

"How's that?"

"If I have this scratch at the dance, the Allendale boys aren't going to be talking about how cute I am. They'll be wondering why there's a giant thirteen scratched on my arm."

"Have you considered long sleeves?"

"Ew, no! And I never will. This is literally a health and hygiene class, and there's nothing healthy or hygienic about a wound that won't heal."

"I'll go with her!" Sadie blurted out, which must have been that impulse the Whisper had told her about. But what was the feeling behind the blurt? What were her instincts urging her to do?

Lindsey flashed Sadie a grateful smile and crooked her fingers into paws and claws. "Thank you," she mouthed. Then to Professor Esther, "A tiger *and* a lion? Come on, nobody's gonna mess with us."

It was then that Sadie realized the purpose of her instinct: it was showing her how to be a good friend.

"Fine, go. You have twenty minutes," the professor said. "Stay together!"

The sky was Tiffany-box blue, the air freshly laundered from the rain. Lindsey lifted her face to the sun and inhaled deeply, savoring every scent, sight, and sound, like a prisoner released. Then she grabbed Sadie by the wrist and said, "Let's make a run for it."

"A run for what?"

"Freedom! We could rescue Kate and the other lights. You know, like those activists who open animal cages and return them to their natural habitats."

Sadie snickered, though she was fairly certain Lindsey was serious. "We need to find those berries and return to *our* natural habitat, or Prof-Esther will—"

"Charm House is not our natural habitat, Sadie," Lindsey said as she tapped a text message into her phone.

It's the closest thing we have right now, Sadie thought. But she didn't want to sound like a chamele-yawn, so she changed the subject. "I can't believe the dance is in two weeks," Sadie said, peeking at Lindsey's phone. *Who is she texting?* "We need a theme."

"We already have one," Lindsey said, still tapping.

"We do?"

"Yeah. Jungle."

"That's not a theme—it's our life."

"We could do a beach theme and wear bathing suits."

Sadie flashed to a vision of herself wearing that poop emoji one-piece in front of the Allendale boys. "Actually, I think your jungle idea is better. Let's stick with that."

"Purrfect." Lindsey's phone dinged with a message. She swiped her lips with gloss and said, "Follow me."

Sadie wondered if she'd ever have the confidence to tell someone to follow her. And if she did, where would she take them?

"Come on, Sadie Lady!" Lindsey called as she began hurtling over rocks and logs, unapologetic and unafraid.

Sadie hesitated, feeling safer on the lawn. But she couldn't stand there while her pack mate ran toward potential danger. *Paws and claws!* "Coming!"

She followed Lindsey through the woods, soothed by the steady beats of her pounding heart. She felt free and alive, like she belonged to everything, and all at once. Until Lindsey stopped running and started sniffing.

"What is it?" Sadie asked, her heart pounding for three new reasons. "Hunters? The Scratcher? IBS?"

"More like ABS," Lindsey purred.

"Huh?"

"Allendale Boys, silly." She pointed up at the three boys perched on the golden-leafed branches of a maple tree, looking like Abercrombie models in their matching uniforms: gray slacks, white shirts, navy cardigans, and red ties. "All clear," Lindsey called.

They jumped down, splashing mud onto their white sneakers—Lindsey wasn't there to pick berries; she was there to pick boys!

"This is Sadie," Lindsey told them. "She's new. This is Link, Colton, and Dean."

No Beak.

They greeted her with lazy waves, which Sadie returned. But could they be trusted? After what Sadie had seen in the infirmary, she wondered if anyone could.

"We're supposed to be back in ten minutes with those berries," she told Lindsey. "We should probably get going."

Ignoring her, Lindsey turned to the tanned boy and said, "Did you bring it, Link?"

"Bring what?" Overgrown hair, dark as his lashes, grazed his eyes like curtains.

"Um, hello, did you forget?"

"Forget?" Link handed her an Allendale yearbook. "You texted me, like, six thousand reminders."

"Hey, Lindsey, check out page twenty-three," Colton snickered.

"Yeah, it's a real *crack*-up," Dean added.

Link flicked Dean on the arm. "It's your fault, dude!"

"How is a picture of your butt crack my fault?"

"I was bending over to pick up *your* phone."

"Was it your missing underwear calling?" Colton teased.

Giggling, Lindsey began flipping through the pages. "Oh, I have to see this!"

"No, you don't!" Link yanked the yearbook from her.

"Give it!" Lindsey insisted.

"No way. You lost your chance."

Lindsey began chasing Link around the maple as the boys cheered her on. Each time she got close to grabbing his collar, he changed direction and escaped.

"That's it!" Lindsey finally said, her flirty tone darkening to frustration. "You're so done." Without warning, she darted up the tree trunk and marked her target. When the time was right, she pounced.

"Whoa, dude!" Colton shouted. Or maybe it was Dean. The shock of it all made the details hard to decipher.

"Get offa me," Link grunted as Lindsey wrested the year-book from his grip.

"Got it!" She dusted off her uniform and stood.

"What just happened?" Link asked, still on the ground. He looked one part confused, three parts impressed.

Colton laughed. "You just got your crack kicked by a girl."

"Or whatever *that* was," Dean muttered, still shocked. "How did you climb up there so fast?"

"*Fast?* That wasn't fast." Lindsey said. "My top speed is—"

"Parkour!" Sadie interrupted. "That's how she did it. We've been studying it in PE. She's the best in the grade." She shot a wide-eyed warning to Lindsey. One more move like that could get them locked up for life. "Why do you want that yearbook so badly, anyway?"

"So the girls can choose dates for the dance."

Link jumped to his feet. "What dance?"

"The Charm House prison guards agreed to let us have a dance," Lindsey said, finger-combing her tiger-striped hair.

"You want to dance with prison guards?"

Lindsey giggled. "No, Lincoln. The dance is with you guys. Your principal is going to announce it today. And I might let you take me if you ditch that dad tie and wear something a little more . . . jungly."

"How's this?" Link began wiggling his butt and loosening his tie, which, Lindsey casually slid from his neck. It was a real movie move. Something a confident character with tons of boy experience might do—nothing Sadie ever expected to see in real life. Especially from a girl her age, a girl who considered Sadie a friend.

"Do we all have to dress jungly, or just Link?" Colton asked.

"All of you," Lindsey said. "That's the theme."

They started growling, roaring, and *eek-eek-eek*ing like monkeys, which Sadie found both cringey and offensive. How would they like it if she talked in a low, mumbly voice and said stupid things like *You want to dance with prison guards?*

"Does anyone know what time it is?" Sadie asked.

Colton checked his Apple watch. "Eleven-fifty-seven."

"Lindsey, we really need to—" The wind blew. Leaves rustled. The grape-eraser smell was back.

"We really need to *what?*" Lindsey wrapped Link's tie around her neck like a scarf.

"Nothing. You stay here. I'll go find the berries."

Sadie followed the scent, picking berries along the way and shoving them into her pockets. She considered taking a moment to admire the purple and white flowers, maybe even thread some through the buttonholes of her uniform. But jump-starting her jumpsuit would have to wait. The grape-eraser smell was intensifying and—

"Hey, Zendaya."

"Oh, hey," Sadie said casually, as if unfazed by his ador-ableness. "Whatcha doin' here?"

111

The Allendale uniform looked different on Beak than it looked on the other boys. His gray pants hung from his hips like they had better things to do, and there were thumb holes in the sleeves of his cardigan. His tie was slung over his shoulder, and his shirt was untucked. Either he had just been attacked by squirrels, or this boy did not want to fit in.

"Some guys ditched third period, and the principal knows. I came to warn them."

"So, technically, you're ditching, too," Sadie said as the effervescent mist danced beneath the surface of her skin.

Beak laughed. "Technically, yes."

An awkward silence filled the space between them. Sadie smoothed her hair. Beak twirled the gold ring on his thumb.

"I have a question," Sadie said. "What's with that ring?" She didn't want to sound rude. But she had never seen a boy her age wearing a ring before, especially on his thumb.

"Is that it?"

"Is that *what*?"

"Your question."

Sadie drew back her head. "I only get one?"

"Yes."

She searched his green eyes for a mischievous flicker or a just-kidding blink. Because she also wanted to know what he'd been hiding behind his back on the day they met, how he'd gotten that C-shaped scar on his cheek, and if his effervescent mist was dancing, too. But there wasn't a single flicker or just-kidding blink to be found. "Wait, are you being serious?"

"Dead."

Sadie giggled. "Why do I only get one question?"

"Is that your question?"

"I'll tell you where your friends are if you give me two questions."

"Wait, you know where they are?"

Sadie grinned. "Is that your question?"

A distant burst of laughter gave Beak all the answers he needed. "Found 'em!" He waved goodbye and took off to find them.

"Wait, don't I get my question first?"

"Is that your question?" he called.

Sadie gave Beak a head start, then followed him, fighting the impulse to unleash her speed and catch up. Fighting so many impulses, actually. Most of them having to do with inviting him to cut class so they could spend the day swapping stories in the woods.

When Sadie finally arrived, Lindsey and Beak were staring at each other, green eyes locked, jaws hanging slack.

"You . . . ," Lindsey said. "I know you." She pressed her temples and doubled over in pain.

Sadie rushed to her side. "Are you okay?"

"My head . . . ," Lindsey mewled.

Beak just stood there, twisting that gold thumb ring while

the others exchanged confused glances. "We have to go!" His voice was urgent and firm. "The bell is about to ring, and Horner is looking for you."

"It just did, actually," Sadie told him.

Colton snickered. "How do you know?"

"I heard it."

"I didn't hear anything," Link said.

"Yeah," Dean said. "How could you have possibly heard that?"

"Oh, I . . . uh . . . I didn't *literally* hear it. I just figured . . ."

"It doesn't matter," Beak said impatiently. "Come on, guys, let's head back." He didn't say goodbye before taking off. He didn't even grunt it. He was just gone.

Seconds later, Lindsey straightened back up and with a bright smile said, "How cute is Link?"

"Are you okay?" Sadie asked.

"Of course I am. Why?" she said as she stuffed the yearbook into her backpack. "Oh, pause!"

Sadie held out her hands and bent her fingers.

Lindsey giggled. "Not *paws.* I meant *pause,* as in, wait a minute, I have something for you." She pulled a necklace out of her backpack and handed it to Sadie—yellow tubular flowers on a leather band, just like hers. "They're cat's claws. They're not real, of course, but they look real, don't they?"

Sadie nodded, unclear on what was happening.

"It was Kate's. It fell off her in the woods during the whole—" Lindsey shook the disturbing thought from her head. "Anyway, Amy brought it back, and I want you to have it."

"Me? Why?"

"Cat power." She fastened it around Sadie's neck and then stood back to admire her work. "It's purrfect."

"Thank you," Sadie beamed as her fingers glided over the strap, then up and down the open petals. It felt like belonging. She wanted to ask if Kate would mind that she was wearing it, why Lindsey's head had hurt when she saw Beak, and why the pain had seemed to stop the moment he left. But Lindsey, giddy from their secret rendezvous, insisted they run back to school before Link realized she'd stolen his tie. So instead of leading, Sadie followed, just like she always did.

fifteen

_L_indsey leaned across her desk and whispered, "Hey, Sadie Lady. Stop biting your nails. It makes us look nervous."

"How does it make _us_ look nervous?" she asked, though she already knew. Her striped nails were Pack black, and she and Lindsey had matching chokers. They were connected now. If one appeared nervous, they both did.

"Something wrong, Miss Samson?" Professor Jo asked.

"No," Sadie lied. Because, yeah, something was very wrong. Amy had spent the night in the infirmary and was supposed to be released in the morning, but she'd missed breakfast and was currently a no-show for Instinct Control. Had her condition worsened? And if so, would Sadie get to apologize for abandoning her? Would she ever have the chance to make things right?

"Since nothing's wrong," Professor Jo said, "why don't you come on up and help with today's lesson?"

"Me?" Sadie asked, hoping that maybe, just maybe, the teacher had been speaking to someone else. Because the last time Sadie had stood at the front of a classroom, she flipped tables, shattered windows, and got herself expelled.

"Fast, fast," Professor Jo said. "Val, Rachel—you, too."

Standing, Sadie tucked her hair behind her ears and then reached for a hood that wasn't there.

Once all three girls were by her side, Professor Jo said, "Today we're going to practice impulse control by way of—" She pointed to the words on the whiteboard.

"Role-playing," the students read aloud.

She beamed. "That's right, role-playing."

Notebooks opened. Pens click-clicked.

"The dance is ten days away," she said, though no one needed reminding. Outfits had been discussed before, during, and after meals. Lindsey and Taylor were booked solid with hair and nail appointments. And the Allendale yearbook had been passed around twice, its pages covered in hearts and sticky notes left by girls laying claim to their future crushes. "That means we have ten days to anticipate possible situations and ten days to learn how to handle them. The more prepared you are, the less vulnerable you will be to your emotions. And the less vulnerable you are to your emotions, the easier it will be to control your—"

"Impulses," everyone said.

"Correct." Professor Jo handed Sadie, Val, and Rachel a sheet of paper that detailed the characters they'd play during the role-playing exercise. Sadie's read:

YOU AND A NICE BOY NAMED JAKE HAVE BEEN HANGING OUT AT THE DANCE. YOU LIKE HIM AND BELIEVE HE LIKES YOU. HE MENTIONS HE'S THIRSTY, AND YOU OFFER TO GET SOME WATER. WHEN YOU COME BACK, JAKE IS HOLDING HANDS WITH MOLLY. WHAT DO YOU DO?

"Ready to begin?" Professor Jo asked.

The girls nodded.

"Annnnd, action!"

Sadie entered the scene holding two imaginary cups of water and approached Jake (Rachel) and Molly (Val). They were close-talking and holding hands.

"What are you doing, Molly?"

"Talking to Jake. What are *you* doing?"

"Bringing him water."

Val took the cup from Sadie's hand. "Aw, that's so sweet of you. Thanks!" She fake gulped Jake's fake water, then handed the fake cup back to Sadie. "I'll take another. With ice."

"I'm not a waitress," Sadie managed with a patient grin.

"You're not?" Val asked. "Then what are you?"

"I'm Jake's friend."

"And I'm Jake's *girl*friend, so leave us alone."

Sadie turned to Jake (Rachel). "You have a girlfriend?"

"Yeah."

"Then why were you all flirty with me?"

Jake (Rachel) shrugged, and in her best guy voice said, "You looked a little desperate, so I decided to keep you company until Molly got here. No one else was going to do it, so . . ."

Sadie's body went slack. Had there been real cups in her hands, they would have crashed to the floor. "What made you think I was desperate?"

Jake (Rachel) reached out her hand and touched Sadie's coarse hair. "That's what."

Their classmates laughed. Suddenly, Sadie was back at Timor Lake Middle being called Hairy Poppins by Sierra and Chloe. The Whisper had told her to find the feeling behind the impulse, but in the moment the only feeling Sadie felt was "RRRRRRAAAAAWWWWRRR!"

Unlike the students at TLM, who had hidden under desks and cowered, the Charm House girls' instincts were to fight back. Rachel, the monkey light, jumped on Sadie's back while Val, Mia, and Liv bared their teeth.

"Cut!" Professor Jo shouted.

"Get off her!" Lindsey pounced toward Sadie, nails swiping.

Chairs screeched as girls jumped up to help.

"CUT!"

Before long a chorus of yips, barks, snarls, hisses, and *eep*s filled the room.

"CUUUUT!" called Professor Jo as she broke up the fight with her eagle-light strength. "Everyone, SIT!"

Once order had been restored and everyone was seated, Professor Jo turned to Sadie. "That is *exactly* what I was worried about!"

"It's not her fault," Lindsey said. "Jake and Molly were seriously mean."

"People can be mean sometimes." Professor Jo glared, the black kohl around her hazel eyes intensifying her conviction. "That doesn't make it okay to fight back."

"Ew! Yes, it does." Lindsey reached for her golden nail file. "We are animal lights, not monsters. What good are these powers if we can't use them to protect ourselves?"

"Sadie wasn't in danger, Lindsey."

"They attacked her hair!"

"With words, not weapons."

"Still," Lindsey said, "they deserved to be put in their place."

"I understand, Lindsey. You've articulated your point well. But if anything like that happens at the dance, you cannot engage."

"So you're saying we should be cowards?"

"No, I'm saying you should be careful. You're stronger, louder, and faster than the boys—"

"Dang straight we are!" Rachel bellowed.

The girls began hissing proudly, and Professor Jo finally cracked a smile. "Bottom line? There's a tremendous amount of strength in—"

"Conflict avoidance," Taylor said, finishing her thought.

"You should know," Lindsey muttered.

"What's *that* supposed to mean?"

"It means Charm House has turned you into a chameleyawn."

The hyena lights giggled.

"Harsh, Linds," Taylor said, her skin turning charcoal gray to match the stone wall behind her.

"Um, camouflage is harder to explain than roaring, don'tcha think?"

Professor Jo sighed. "You can't keep fighting this, Lindsey."

"Watch me."

They glared at each other, eyes locked in a silent standoff, until the click of the classroom door distracted them.

Professor Jo turned. "Taylor, are you trying to sneak out of here?"

"I need to go to the bathroom," Taylor said, still invisible.

"Can you hold it? We're discussing something important here."

"She can't," Lindsey explained. "She's a nervous pee-er."

The door clicked shut, and Professor Jo lowered her gaze. "The more things change . . ."

"The more they stay the same," Lindsey said.

Professor Jo's eyebrows shot up. "How did you know that?"

Lindsey began blinking, her expression a flash of familiarity followed by a pinch of pain, just like she'd felt when she saw Beak. "My head!" she cried as she doubled over.

"Lindsey, what's happening?" Professor Jo asked, rushing to her side.

"It hurrrrts!"

"When's the last time you took your elixir?"

"This morning."

"Well, you need more."

"The elixir is for memory loss, not headaches," Sadie reminded her.

"Right, yes, right," Professor Jo said, hands shaking.

"I'll take her to Nurse Walker," Sadie offered.

"Fine, yes, go. Hurry!"

Sadie helped Lindsey to her feet and guided her out the door. When they stepped into the hallway, Lindsey let out a sharp gasp.

"Don't worry," Sadie cooed. "All we have to do is walk down the hall, and the nurse will make you feel better, okay?"

Lindsey didn't move. She just stood there pointing at the floor—at Taylor, who was lying unconscious with the number 13 scratched onto her calf, and Amy was standing over her, blinking innocently, as if she had no clue what had happened. Which even Sadie found hard to believe.

sixteen

It was 7:45 on a school night—a time when girls gathered in the Watering Hole to swap gossip and share stolen cookies from dinner. Instead, Sadie was circling her room like a trapped zoo animal, biting her nubby nails.

Since Taylor's attack, a pall of fear had fallen over Charm House. The Caf—once a lively symphony of chatter—was now a screechy dirge of scraping forks and clattering cups. Silence was the new sound. Paranoia, the new pastime. Confusion, the new cardio. And Sadie, who was finally starting to fit in, was freaking out. Who was doing this? Who was next? And why?

Whether Amy was innocent or guilty, Sadie missed her. Her clumsiness was charming; her guidance, comforting. At the same time, Sadie was relieved that Miss Flora had moved her to a secret location for questioning. Because loneliness aside, the alibi Amy had tried to sell was a little hard to buy.

She claimed that Nurse Walker had wanted to run a few more tests before releasing her from the infirmary; Amy even showed her late slip as proof. Then, while on her way to Instinct Control, she saw Taylor passed out in the hallway with a number 13 on her calf. Amy froze, just as she had when Kate was taken by the hunters. And that's when Lindsey and Sadie showed up. Minutes later, Miss Flora arrived on the scene and asked if Amy had seen anything unusual.

"No!" she cried. "Taylor must have been in camo mode; she just appeared on the floor out of nowhere."

That part was true. Taylor was camouflaged when she left Instinct Control. Which certainly made a case for Amy's innocence—how could she scratch what she couldn't see? But if Amy hadn't done it, who had?

Sadie tried listening for that voice inside her—the one that seemed to know things before she did. But like everyone at Charm House these days, it wasn't saying much. Forget instincts; she needed facts.

She asked the quilts on Amy's bed, the rows of photographs and birthday cards taped to her wall. They'd known her longer; maybe they'd have some insight. But before they could offer any, Miss Flora's voice came over the loudspeaker.

"Good evening," she said, hours after the attack. "As you know, three of our students have suffered untenable acts of aggression, and the person responsible is still out there. Trust that we are doing everything we can to find them, and when we do, they will pay for what they've done."

On the other side of Sadie's door, girls hissed their approval.

"Until then, the following rules will be enforced: Everyone is required to shelter in place; that means you stay in your rooms with the doors locked. No. Visiting. Allowed. You may only leave for meals and quick trips to the Watering Hole, and professors will be stationed in the hallways to escort you. For the time being, Prowl Passes will be revoked, and the Allendale dance has been canceled."

"Are you kidding me right now?" Lindsey shouted.

Others began shouting, too.

"Everyone please vacate the Watering Hole and return to your rooms," Miss Flora continued, oblivious to the fallout. "Curfew begins in ten minutes. Thank you for your cooperation, and remember: if you see something, say something."

Girls began shouting about injustice and wanting their tuition money back, but Sadie was too despondent to join them. No more dance planning meetings with Lindsey and Taylor. No more tree-climbing lessons. No more visits to the Den. And no more Beak. She had finally been learning how to tap into her power and now they were in lockdown.

"It's not fair," Mia whined. "You-know-who is going to get attacked next."

"You think?" Val said.

"Whoever is doing this is obviously targeting the Pack and she's the only one left, so why not make her shelter in place and let the rest of us go free?"

"Because Miss Flora is afraid of her, that's why," said Rachel. "Did you hear her roar in class? That girl has zero instinct control. Imagine how mad she'd be if she was the only one who had to miss the dance?"

"It's so unfair."

"I know. Just let her get scratched so we can move on."

Sadie clapped a hand over her mouth and lowered onto her bed. They were talking about *her*.

Lindsey growled. "You want Sadie to get scratched?"

"Don't you?" Val said. "Because of her our dance is canceled."

"This is not her fault!"

"You're just saying that to keep her out of trouble."

"Why would I do that?"

"To protect yourself from us," Mia said. "Kate is gone and Taylor's in the infirmary, sooo *pee-pee hazard* alert."

"What's pee-pee hazard?" Lindsey asked, annoyed.

Liv snickered. "It's another way of saying—"

"*Urine trouble!*" Val and Mia bellowed.

Lindsey scoffed, "Um, hello, I'm not in trouble, and I don't need protection."

"Then why is Sadie Pack-marked?"

"Pack-marked?" Lindsey asked, feigning innocence, but

even Sadie knew what Mia meant. The black nail stripes, Kate's necklace, a seat at the Pack's table, and an-all access pass to their dorm room. "She's not marked, Val. She's my friend."

Sadie's insides warmed. The tiger had her back.

"You have to admit, things have gotten even worse now that she's here."

"The only thing I'll admit, Mia, is that you need to shave your legs. You're even hairier than Rachel."

The gong sounded and Miss Flora's voice returned. "Curfew has begun. Everyone to your rooms. I repeat, curfew has begun."

Once the hallways were silent, Sadie pressed her mouth against the wall and whispered into Lindsey's room, "I heard that, you know."

"Ignore them," she whispered back.

"How? They think I'm next."

"Don't listen to them," Lindsey said as she flicked on her sleep machine. The sound of crickets filled the room. "Night-night, Sadie Lady."

"Wait, that's *it*?"

"It's beauty-sleep time."

Sadie rolled her eyes. On a bad day, Lindsey looked like a Neutrogena model. On a good day, Neutrogena models wanted to look like her. "Aren't you worried?"

"About looking ugly? Yes, very."

"No, about who did this and who they're going to get next."

"Not really. You're doing all the worrying for me."

"Lindsey, this isn't funny. Everyone is going to think it's my fault the dance was canceled."

"That's why we're going to un-cancel it."

"How?"

"We'll riot and protest until Miss Flora changes her mind." Lindsey yawned. "But I can't organize a rebellion if I'm tired, so let me sleep, lion." She turned up the volume on the sound machine. The conversation was over.

I'm not a lion, Sadie thought. *I'm a lemming. Lions are leaders and all I know how to do is follow.*

The Whisper said leading was about uniting people who believed in a mutual cause and helping them achieve it. Did they even *have* a mutual cause? Everyone at Charm House was so cliquey and divided. Speciesist, as Amy put it. Was there any one thing they agreed on? And then it hit her: *The dance! They all wanted the dance.*

Sadie returned to the wall and knocked. "Lindsey, I have an idea!" It was super risky and not thought through at all. But it would unite the girls for a mutual cause and prove to them, and to Sadie herself, that she had what it took to lead. "Wake up!"

All she heard was crickets.

"I know how to unite everyone!"

More crickets.

"Let's sneak out of here and . . ."

The crickets got quieter. "And *what*?"

"Have a secret dance."

"How would we do that?"

"I have no idea."

"What if we're taken by IBS?"

"Uh . . ." Sadie's stomach dipped. She hadn't thought about that. "Safety in numbers, right?"

"We'd be in violation of every Charm House rule," Lindsey asked. "You know that, right?"

"Yeah."

"If we get busted, we could get expelled."

Sadie was doubtful that Miss Flora would actually kick anyone out of school. It wasn't safe out there. "Maybe, but—"

"Purrfect," Lindsey said. "Count me in!"

seventeen

*A*fter one week of sheltering in place, online classes, and YouTube exercise videos, the thought of spending another minute caged up in her room terrified Sadie more than hunters, Scratchers, or Miss Flora. It was time—specifically, 11:45 on Friday night—and the Secret Twilight Undercover Dance, or Operation: STUD, as Sadie called it, was officially underway.

Without her Prowl Passes, Sadie had nothing to do at night but study the routines of the security team that patrolled the hallways. She'd learned that:

1. The guards packed up at 11:53 p.m.
2. At 11:55 p.m., they headed home.
3. At 11:55 the new guards were in the Caf, loading up on coffee and pastries.
4. That left roughly five minutes of unpatrolled hallway time for Sadie and the girls to sneak out.
5. Starting NOW!

Sadie lifted a hand to the wall and signaled Lindsey with two snaps: *Text Link*.

"Done," Lindsey whispered.

Sadie's pulse quickened. This was really happening. "Cue the giraffe lights. Tell them to reposition the ceiling cameras and then meet us—"

"We're on it."

"Gia?"

"You can talk to us directly, Sadie. Our hearing is just as good as yours."

"Yeah," added Jasmine. "We've been listening to you plan this thing all week."

"Same," squeaked Sondra, the rat light. "I put the *ear* in *hear*, you know." Then, "Aaa-choo!" She sniffled. "And the sneeze in allergies."

Sadie giggled, overcome by a warm wave of love for these quirky creatures. Despite their enviable powers, they struggled in ways that most Typicals couldn't possibly understand. And that shared struggle bonded them for life.

"Once Gia and Jasmine have repositioned the cameras," Sadie continued, "they'll give an all-clear hiss, and you'll—"

"Use my agile body to slip under everyone's doors and tell them to meet in Rachel and Piper's room," Sondra said. "At that point, the monkey lights will have one minute to open the window, form the Charm House chain we practiced during the fire drill, and get to the ground. The hyena lights will toss out two mattresses, the monkey lights will position them, and we'll jump. Then everyone meets at the tree houses, and we'll head into the woods together." Sondra blew her nose. "Told you I could hear."

A second wave of warmth purled through Sadie, this one because the girls were actually going along with her plan. The feeling was a mix of power and panic. Like the chocolate-and-vanilla soft-serve she always got at the Spotted Owl, the flavors swirled together, making it hard to taste one without the other.

Fifteen minutes later, the girls had gathered safely below the tree houses, white plumes of air trailing from their glossy mouths as they hissed in honor of Sadie and her purrfect plan.

Had the adventure ended there—with dozens of glitter-dusted girls praising Sadie while a crescent moon lit the night with its silver smile of approval—she would have said it was the best moment of her life. But the adventure was only just beginning. "Is everyone ready?"

"*We're* ready, but ew . . ." Lindsey snarled at Sadie's black leggings and matching hoodie. "You're not." She handed Sadie a pink garment bag. "Surprise!"

Sadie took a step back, suddenly convinced that she was being set up, that she was really the butt of some humiliating prank designed by Lindsey to keep Sadie from usurping her power. "What is that?"

"Open it." Lindsey beamed. Her hair, which had been artfully twisted into a crown bun and fastened with Link's necktie, seemed swollen with bad intentions. "Go on."

Hands shaking, Sadie slowly reached for the opening of the garment bag, but Lindsey, impatient, unzipped it herself.

"It's not a hoodie kind of night," she said, revealing a silky pink T-shirt with the shoulders cut out and a denim skirt with a nail file in the pocket and gold studs down the side. "Studs in honor of STUD." She smiled proudly. "Get it?"

Sadie nodded, because saying yes would have made her cry. *So this is what it feels like to have a true friend,* she thought while changing into her new outfit. It was like a crush without all the insecurity and distraction—a person to call home.

Rocking the kind of confidence one can get only from wearing someone else's much better clothes, Sadie and Lindsey—with their matching cat's claw necklaces and black-striped nails—led everyone to the clearing. Behind them, girls chatted giddily about boys they couldn't wait to see and the risks they were taking to do so, paying no mind to the skeletal tree branches or the rustling leaves that normally would have terrified them into turning around.

"I can't believe Taylor is stuck in the infirmary." Lindsey sighed. "She would have loved this."

Sadie stopped and cocked her head. "You think?"

"Um, no! She would have nervous-peed her pants, like, twenty times by now."

"A cha-pee-leon!" Sadie blurted, sending her and Lindsey into hysterics.

Did she feel bad making a joke at her pack mate's expense? Yes. Especially since Taylor had been hurt and was missing all the fun. But Taylor would not have been okay with such a high-risk adventure. And Sadie, who was having the best night of her life, was not okay with that.

They arrived at the clearing before the boys, which was part of the plan. Decorations needed to be hung, music needed to be cued, and lips needed to be reglossed. The hyena lights moved boulders from the dance floor, the giraffe lights hung colorful socks from tree branches, and everyone else pulled stolen Caf snacks from their backpacks and arranged them on tables made from fallen logs. Lindsey scooted up the trunk of a maple tree, tied a volleyball covered in pieces of broken mirror to a branch, then gave her makeshift disco ball a smack. Fragments of chrome-colored light danced merrily around the woods.

"Better than the Charm House gym, don'tcha think?" Lindsey said as she shimmied down.

"It's purrfect," Sadie said, referring not only to the dancing light but also to the collective bravery and cooperation of the girls who had dared to make it all possible. After years of loneliness, she would finally have a real story of friendship to tell. One of approval and acceptance, of learning how to stand out and fit in at the same time. Yes, she was risking everything for this adventure, they all were, and that shared struggle would bond them for life. In a way, playing it safe and passing up a chance for that bond felt like the bigger risk. One that Sadie was not willing to take.

The song "Dance Monkey" blasted from the speakers. "Who's ready to par-tayyyy?" Rachel shouted.

Corrina covered her sensitive ears. "It's too loud!"

"If anything's too loud, it's your dress," Rachel said. "That plaid is bad!"

"How can you even see? It's so dark out here," Rio said. She was a lizard light whose thick glasses were clearly not thick enough. "I know! Let's make a fire!"

"I know!" mocked Piper. "Let's draw attention to ourselves!"

"Oh, and the music isn't drawing attention?" Corrina snipped.

"Not as much as your dress."

"Shhhh!" Sadie snapped. "They're coming. . . ."

Just then a band of boys appeared from the opposite side of the clearing—a tableau of prep-school cool in their casual T-shirts and weekend jeans. Sadie began fidgeting nervously while others giggled. The crisp night air turned electric, and the girls, like corn kernels in a microwave, were ready to pop. Still, they kept to one side of the clearing while the boys kept to the other—a childish reaction that Lindsey had zero patience for.

"Let's dance!" she called. Then, peace fingers pointing at the stars, she twirled over to Link, grabbed him by a belt loop, and yanked him into the center of the dance floor with a little too much force.

"Easy, tiger!" He laughed, thrown by her strength.

A few girls exchanged concerned glances. But if Lindsey was rattled by Link's spot-on comment, she didn't show it. Instead, she continued to yank and dance, forcing everyone to shed their inhibitions and make up for years of lost party time. Soon arms were waving, booties were shaking, and boys were being flung by girls who didn't know the power of their own strength—all as a pungent waft of Axe body spray and magazine perfume samples rose from their sweaty bodies and hovered above them like a rain cloud.

And then there was Beak, standing on the sidelines, kicking rocks with his navy Converse sneaks, eyes downcast as if he wanted to be left alone.

Sadie's heart began to race. She could feel it thumping against her teeth, her ears, her scalp. She wanted to run to him and away from him at the same time. But what did Beak want? Was he as shy and hoping she'd make the first move? Or did he loathe wild dance parties in the woods and double loathe girls who organized them? Lindsey would have grabbed him. Taylor would have made herself invisible. And Sadie? Well, Sadie had no idea what she'd do. Everything about this night was a first.

While contemplating her next move, Sasha playfully butt-bumped Dean and accidentally sent him hurtling across the dance floor. Dean smashed into Colton, who smashed into Jasmine, who smashed into a redheaded boy, who smashed into Sadie, who lost her footing and smashed into Beak's grapiness.

"Hey, Zendaya," he said, amused by her clumsy arrival.

"Uh, hey, Frodo."

His green eyes narrowed. "Frodo?"

Sadie pointed to the gold band around his thumb. *"The Lord of the Rings."*

Beak laughed.

Sadie exhaled.

Beak glanced down at his shoes.

Sadie glanced up at the moon.

Beak peeked at Sadie.

Sadie peeked at Beak.

Silence, awkward and mocking, calcified between them.

"So . . . why are you standing around kicking rocks?" Sadie finally asked.

"I, uh—" His attention shifted to whatever was going on behind her back. "What's that about?"

Sadie turned to find Lindsey lifting Link over her head, figure-skater-style.

"Oh no . . ."

"How can that possibly be . . . possible?"

"Parkour training," Sadie answered. What was Lindsey thinking? It was like she *wanted* to get caught.

"You should probably warn her."

Sadie's skin flushed, and not in the fun, crushy sort of way. "About what?"

"Uh, head trauma. That can't be safe."

"Yes. Right. Agreed. I'll do that," Sadie said, confused. If Beak was so concerned, why send her? Why not warn Link and Lindsey himself? Unless . . . what if this wasn't about safety at all? What if he was trying to get rid of her so he could hang out with his real crush? Just like in Professor Jo's exercise.

Dizzy from the possibility, Sadie stumbled toward Lindsey, consumed by panic. She wanted to give every crushing couple that had been dancing around her an envious shove. After that she would give Professor Jo's stupid exercise two shoves. One for making her doubt Beak and another for making her want to shove in the first place. Wasn't Charm House supposed to cure her of all that?

"There you are!" Lindsey called. She reached for Sadie's hand and drew her into the madness. "This night is so *un*!"

"Un-fun?"

"No, un*believable*! And it's all because of you! Well, and me. But you, too. Cat power!" She let out a hearty, liberating roar.

The dingoes backed her up with a series of howls. Val,

Liv, and Mia began yipping. Rachel and Piper *eep*ed. Soon a chorus of jungle sounds punctured their fruit-and-sweat-scented force field and ricocheted off the stars.

"Quiet, you guys!" Sadie urged. Had they lost their minds? "What are you doing?" Embarrassed, but mostly afraid, she glanced back at Beak, hoping that he was somehow oblivious to the chaos. But he was gone.

What if he'd been turned off by their immature display? Or worse! What if he'd figured out who they were and was calling IBS?

"Beak!" Sadie called, her voice tight and desperate. "Beak?"

Senses sharpening, Sadie set out to track his scent, but the dance party musk was too overpowering. "Beak? Where are you?"

She eventually found him slumped up against a tree, his body rag-doll limp and his eyes fighting to stay open. Sadie ran toward him semi-blind with panic—panic that intensified when she saw the number 13 scratched into his arm. "Lindsey!" she screamed. "Someone! Help!"

Lindsey was the first to arrive on the scene, but the moment she saw Beak, she clutched her head and backed away.

"Sadie did this?" Mia said to no one in particular.

"What? No!" Sadie screeched. "I found him this way. We have to get him to the nurse. Link? Colton? Someone help me lift him," she said.

But it was too late. The Allendale boys ran north, the

Charm House girls ran south, and Lindsey, who hadn't even bothered saying goodbye, was long gone.

Some leader, Sadie thought of herself as she hoisted Beak over her shoulder. The only place she had led them was straight into danger. And that special bond she had with the girls—the one Sadie thought would last a lifetime and never be broken?

SNAP!

eighteen

"**I**'m not Frodo," Beak mumbled as Sadie carried him through the darkness, his shoulder grinding against her flower necklace, her denim skirt bunching up around her legs.

"If you're not Frodo," Sadie said with a grunt, "who are you?" She was trying to keep him talking, because that's what people always did in the movies.

"I'm Hol-zen Caulfield from *Casher in th' Rye*," he slurred.

"The book?"

"Yesss."

"Why Holden?" she asked, though the real question was, *Where am I going?* Taking Beak to Charm House would put everyone at risk of exposure. But if she took him to Allendale, the principal would send him to the hospital. Questions about the number 13 and its significance would invite an unwanted investigation. The press would get involved. Then IBS. At least Nurse Walker and Miss Flora had experience with this; they'd know how to revive him.

Sadie, on the other hand, was a lost cause. Breaking the

shelter-in-place order was one thing, but showing up with a semiconscious private-school boy on her back was quite another. Expulsion was inevitable, incarceration possible. But abandoning him the way his cowardly so-called friends had was not an option.

"Why are you Holden?" Sadie asked again.

"Holzen's ister Phoebe stahnz on the carousel horse ta reash da brass ring," he slurred. "He'z cared she'll fall but haz ta let her try. I hadda let my ister try, too."

"You have a sister?" Sadie panted.

"Nah 'nymore."

A stampede of worst-case scenarios bum-rushed Sadie's mind. "What happened?" she dared.

Beak didn't answer. Instead, his warm breath hit the nape of her neck in shallow bursts. It was a level of intimacy that, under normal circumstances, would have twisted Sadie into an emotional, hormonal hair ball. But in that moment, all she felt was panic.

"D'ju see that?" he suddenly asked.

"See what?"

"Lin'sey lifted Link o'er her head and . . ." Beak drifted off for a minute and then said, "I called Mom. It'safe. . . ."

"What's safe?" Sadie pressed, determined to keep him talking, no matter how nonsensical his words were.

He didn't respond. She gave him a jostle. "Beak?" She jostled him again. "Talk to me!"

He didn't say another word. His breath against Sadie's neck was the only proof that he was still alive.

———————

Sadie arrived at the iron gates breathless and shaking, prepared for Miss Flora's wrath. She'd put the *harm* in *Charm* when she organized STUD. She deserved the very worst. Instead, it was Professor Jo waiting at the door, her body wrapped in a red kimono, her features clenched with concern.

"I'm so sorry," Sadie began, tears pinching the backs of her eyes. "I didn't mean for anyone to get hurt."

Hands shaking, Professor Jo lifted Beak off Sadie and cradled his lanky body in her arms. As heavy and cumbersome as he was, Sadie instantly missed the weight of him. Would she ever feel it again?

"He was conscious when I found him . . . ," Sadie said, her cheeks now streaked with tears.

Without so much as a nod of acknowledgment, Professor Jo whisked him inside, leaving Sadie alone with the one-armed Virgin Mary statue that hung above the door. *Now we're both busted,* it seemed to say.

Desperate to fix what she had broken, Sadie hurried after Professor Jo, her cries of apology echoing off the stone walls. But the professor never even looked back. When she arrived at the infirmary, Miss Flora was already there. Together, they laid Beak on a cot while Nurse Walker began poking his wan skin with needles. The cot beside his was curtained off. It must have been Taylor's.

"Say something, Brett!" Miss Flora begged as she and Professor Jo stroked his forehead.

"You know his name?" Sadie asked from the open doorway.

The women turned.

"What are you doing here?" Miss Flora snapped.

"I'm the one who found him. I brought him back."

"I'm sensing a real pattern here, Miss Samson."

Sadie resisted the urge to defend herself. It was not the time. "He *was* talking. . . ."

Miss Flora and Professor Jo exchanged a look of concern.

"Something about *The Catcher in the Rye* and Holden Caulfield. How his sister reached for the brass ring and—"

"Sister?"

"Holden's."

"Oh." Miss Flora sighed as if relieved. "We'll take it from here, Sadie. Go directly to your room and get some rest."

Rest? Sadie couldn't rest on a good night. Did they really expect her to nod off after *this*?

"Let me help," Sadie tried. "I'll stay up and watch him. . . ."

"Now!"

With that, Miss Flora turned her attention back to Beak, making it painfully clear that Sadie no longer mattered.

nineteen

*I*nstead of going back to her room, Sadie made a mad dash for the one place that could help her deal with, well, everything: the guilt, the shame, the confusion, the abandonment. . . . When combined, those feelings weighed more than one thousand Beaks and Amys. Sadie was strong, but not *that* strong. She needed help.

Using the nail file Lindsey had slipped into the back pocket of her denim skirt, Sadie picked the lock on the spa door and slipped inside. Padding through the eucalyptus-scented steam, she followed the sound of the waterfall to the rainbow-colored pond and took a moment to delight in its bizarre beauty. Had she not been deserted by her so-called friends, Sadie might have been tempted to share this with them. But not anymore. It was the only place in her world that felt betrayal-free, and she wanted to keep it that way.

Like last time, Sadie placed her palm on the rock and marveled as the water turned to sand. When the Den door slid open, the crushing weight of her feelings subsided a teensy bit. Help was on the way.

"Hello?" she called into the darkness. No one answered. She kept calling, refusing to believe that her last hope was hopeless. "Hello? Anyone there?"

Still nothing.

Sadie's shoulders sagged. *Not you, too.*

Tears began to flood her eyes, then, *whoosh!* The smoke-less fire ignited, and the Den came alive.

"Long night?" the Whisper asked.

Sadie snickered at the understatement as she collapsed onto the pillows. Then, with a heavy sigh, she said, "I quit."

This time it was the Whisper who snickered. "What, exactly, are you quitting?"

"Leading, or whatever it is I'm supposed to be doing." Sadie rolled onto her side. "I'm done."

"Something happened," the Whisper said, like she already knew.

"I tried to bring everyone together—that's what happened."

"And then?"

"Everything fell apart." Sadie gazed at the fire, envying how freely it danced. "Now everyone is in trouble, Beak got hurt, and . . . and . . ." Fresh tears began to fall. "They just left me there!" She began to sob.

"Those are good reasons to be upset."

Sadie nodded.

"Which is the biggest?"

"The biggest what?"

"Reason," the Whisper said. "Which part hurt you the most? And tell the truth. I'll know if you're lying."

"How?"

"Put your hand on your heart."

Sadie did. The rhythm was steady but sad.

"The beats quicken when you're lying. Typicals need electrodes or stethoscopes to gather that data. Lights just have to listen for it."

Sadie sat up, inspired by the potential of her newfound gift. Police would pay her billions of dollars to interrogate suspects. Shopaholics would invite her on mall sprees to keep greedy salespeople from fake flattering. And she'd never get tricked into believing someone had her back again.

"So, what's your answer, Sadie? What hurt you the most? Was it the pain you caused others or the pain they caused you?"

"The pain I caused others, duh!" Sadie would have said, had the Whisper not tipped her off to the beating lie detector inside her chest. But now that honesty was her only policy, she shamefully muttered, "The pain they caused me."

"Then bringing everyone together was not your true goal. Popularity was. And that's not a worthy goal."

"It is when you don't have any friends," Sadie countered. "Whatever. You don't get it."

The Whisper said, "Hmmm," like someone who absolutely did. "When your sole intention is to get someone else's approval, you're setting yourself up for disappointment."

"Well, that's super depressing."

"It's also super true. You can't control other people's reactions, and most times the one they give you is not the one you wanted."

"Meaning?" Sadie asked, more confused than ever.

"The only person on the planet you can control is yourself."

Sadie rolled her eyes. Why did grown-ups always talk like fortune cookies?

"I'm not trying to control anyone," Sadie said. "I just want . . ." She paused to wipe away a new stream of tears. "I just want real friends."

"Then *act* like a real friend."

"I did! And they ditched me anyway."

"Keep doing it. Be the example. Be kindness and loyalty and support. Don't stop. In time, the girls who stand for the same things will step into your light, and the ones who don't will hide from it. But no more sneaking out. That was just stupid, not to mention dangerous."

Sadie smiled a little; it was funny getting schooled by a whisper. It also felt like being loved.

"Now go. The breakfast gong is about to sound, and you'd better be in your room when it does."

"I'm not going to breakfast."

"You get what you are, Sadie. Be great and you'll get great," the Whisper said. Then the fire went out and the Den went dark.

twenty

That morning, the girls woke to Miss Flora's less-than-pleased voice over the loudspeaker.

"I have yet to find words to describe how I feel about last night's unconscionable caper. And until the ringleader of said caper steps forward and accepts responsibility, you, my dear Charm House girls, will not have words, either. Because in addition to the shelter-in-place order, I will be enforcing a schoolwide ban on talking, so that plans such as the one you hatched last night can no longer be shared. The only sound I will accept from now on is silence and the only words that can break that silence are *It. Was. Me.* Good day."

Sadie kept her head down during their silent march to the Caf; she kept it down as she piled bacon onto her tray; and she kept it down when she walked past her ex-friends and sat alone. Anything to avoid the blame darts they were shooting from their vengeful eyes. Because it was no secret. Sadie *was* the ringleader, but technically weren't they all?

It's not like she had to beg the girls to go along with the

plan. They were a team! They'd wanted STUD just as much as she had. At least it had felt that way at the time. But as Miss Flora once said, feelings aren't facts. And the fact was, they abandoned her. And now, instead of offering Sadie a hand and helping her up, they wanted her to take the fall. The Whisper was right: the only person she could control was herself. And that self was never going to make eye contact with anyone again. It also wasn't going to care about paws, claws, packs, pacts, matching necklaces, or—

"Don't bite," breathed a familiar voice. It was Lindsey. She was sitting with Gia and Jasmine, a mug pressed to her lips, pretending to sip.

Sadie kept right on biting. If she wanted to nibble her nails into nubs, she would.

"About leaving you . . . ," Lindsey whispered. "I didn't have a choice."

Sadie began scraping the black polish off her thumbnail. *There's always a choice.*

"It's that Beak guy. The second I saw him, I got a terrible headache."

Sadie's stomach dipped at the thought of Beak in the infirmary. It dipped again when she considered the fun they might have had if none of this had happened. What about Taylor? Was she doing any better? And where were they keeping Amy?

"You have to believe me, Sadie Lady. I never would have bailed if my head—"

Ms. Finkle smacked a hand on the table. "Silence, Miss Striker! One more word and you'll be eating in your room."

A slow smile curled across Sadie's lips. *Take that, tiger! Maybe next time you won't use me for hyena protection. Maybe next time you won't bolt at the first sign of trouble. Maybe next time you won't leave me to carry my semiconscious crush through the woods— alone! AT NIGHT!*

As if she could hear those thoughts, Lindsey turned to Sadie and with a hand to her heart, mouthed, "I'm sorry."

Sadie listened for the sound of Lindsey's heartbeat. If it was speeding, she'd know the apology wasn't sincere. But it was useless. Hearts were beating all around her. Isolating Lindsey's was impossible.

More than anything, Sadie wanted to believe that Lindsey was telling the truth. She'd had a taste of real friendship and never wanted to live without it again. But headache or not, Lindsey had abandoned her. So the question wasn't whether to believe her; it was, would you rather (A) be completely friendless or (B) have friends you don't trust?

Sadie's answer was (A)—she would rather be completely friendless. She was already used to feeling lonely, and it left zero room for disappointment. It was the safer option.

Sadie was about to turn her back on Lindsey—*apology not accepted!*—when she heard the waterfall. She glanced around, assuming the others heard it, too. But eyes remained lowered and forks continued to clink. It was as if the Whisper was trying to send her a message, or maybe a reminder: *I'm here. . . . Don't forget about me.*

Sadie thought of their conversation—the Whisper telling her to be the example of friendship, to be great and she'd get great, to stand up for what she believed in. Was it fortune cookie advice? Yes. But it was the only advice Sadie had. And with everything else gone, she had nothing to lose.

Without another thought, Sadie surrendered to her instincts and pushed back her chair. The sudden screech ripped through the silence in the Caf, and everyone turned.

"Sit, Miss Samson," Ms. Finkle said.

Sadie stood. "It. Was. Me," she announced. "I was the ringleader. This is all my fault."

Forks stopped clinking. The room grew hot.

Ms. Finkle smiled wryly. "Very well, then. I'll text Miss Flora and—"

Her words were interrupted by another screech. It was Lindsey's chair this time. "It. Was. Me," she said. "I'm the ringleader."

Sadie's jaw slackened.

"No. It. Was. Me. I'm the ringleader," Gia said, standing.

"It. Was. Me," Sondra said. "I'm the ringleader."

Piper stood. "No, me."

"No, me," Rachel said.

"They're lying," Corrina said. "It was me. You should probably send me home."

Before long, every girl in the Caf was standing, along with the hairs on Sadie's arms.

When Miss Flora arrived, she adjusted her red-framed glasses and took in the scene. "If you're all responsible for the crime, you'll all do the time. No Wi-Fi for a month and . . . and . . . and . . . no dessert!"

The girls exchanged victorious smiles.

"Don't even *think* about talking!" Ms. Finkle blasted.

The celebration was silent, but their pride was loud. They may have lost Wi-Fi and dessert, but those were small prices to pay for the unbreakable bond they finally shared.

"Thank you," Sadie mouthed.

Lindsey curled her fingers into claws. Sadie curled back.

Their feud was over, but the real battle was just getting started. The Scratcher was still at large, Amy was not part of the Pack, and Sadie had never gotten to dance with Beak. Until those battles were fought—and won—the lion inside Sadie would not rest.

twenty-one

Encouraged by Sadie's confession and the fact that there hadn't been a scratch in five days, Miss Flora loosened her social restrictions, allowing the girls one hour to socialize after dinner. And the timing couldn't have been better. Taylor had just been released from the infirmary, and Sadie wanted answers.

"How do you not remember *anything*?" she asked for what had to have been the fifteenth time. Because, come on. *Nothing?*

She was next door in Lindsey and Taylor's room, surrounded by the wilting wildflowers and glittery get-well cards that had accumulated during Taylor's recovery.

"All I know is, one minute I'm leaving Instinct Control," Taylor said as Lindsey painted fresh black stripes on her nails. "And the next, Nurse Walker is waving smelling salts under my nose."

"Do you remember seeing Amy before it happened?"

"I don't remember *seeing her* seeing her." Taylor squinted

as if searching the dark corners of her brain. "But I sensed her. Just like I sensed that she framed Kate—"

"Pause," Sadie said.

Taylor and Lindsey raised their palms and bent their fingers.

"No." Sadie laughed. "Not *paws*. *Pause*. As in hold on a second. Amy can't be the Scratcher. She was a victim, too. It doesn't add up."

Sadie leaned back on her elbows. "Maybe it wasn't a student. Maybe it was Miss Flora. You know, to scare us into following the rules."

"Or Nurse Walker. To get more business."

"Or Ms. Finkle, to cut down on cafeteria noise."

"Pause," Lindsey said, ears perked, spine stiff.

Sadie and Taylor arched their fingers.

"Other kind," she whispered. "Hear that?"

Rubber-soled sneakers squeaked against the hallway floor. The footsteps were getting louder, closer . . . and then the door handle jiggled.

Sadie and Lindsey sprang to their feet. Taylor became invisible.

"Who's there?" Lindsey called.

"Elixir time," Miss Flora said.

Lindsey opened the door with a reluctant sigh. "Coming."

"I might as well go, too," Taylor said, still invisible. "Gotta hit the restroom before the Watering Hole. I'm a total cha-pee-leon these days."

Sadie bristled. "What did you just say?"

"Corny dad joke, sorry. Back in a sec."

Alone in their room with Lindsey's vast nail polish collection sprawled out in front of her, Sadie began painting paws and claws on her uniform. She made the paws black and each claw a different color. Mostly to represent the variety of species at Charm House, but also as a tribute to the rainbow pond—and the secret sanctuary that had helped her find her way.

While contemplating pinks—Super Bossa Nova or Lovie Dovie—Sadie felt a pinch on the side of her neck. She smacked the spot, hoping to squish whatever it was, then checked her hand to examine her kill. Aside from a few nail polish smudges, nothing was there.

Sadie scanned the room, hoping to trap the insect before it got her again, when everything around her became fuzzy. She tried blinking it all back into focus, but once her lids were closed, they refused to pop back open. Her shoulders began to tingle. Her head, suddenly bowling ball–heavy, rolled to the right, then the left, then it tipped forward, and then—

Sadie's eyes fluttered open. A very blurry Lindsey was swinging Link's red tie and—

Someone was growling. Someone else was whimpering. Sadie wished they would keep it down so she could go back to sleeeee—

The smell was sharp and arresting, with a note of fruitiness, and it woke Sadie with a start.

"Wha's appening?" she slurred. A girl was kneeling in front of her, waving a bottle under Sadie's nose. Sadie blinked her into focus. "Lin-sey?"

"It worked!" Lindsey said. "Gotta love nail polish remover."

"Ew, no, I don't," Sadie moaned as she lazy-waved the bottle, and its offending blue liquid, away from her face. "Is that Taylor?" she asked, referencing the girl with the Mohawk, who was bound to the leg of Lindsey's bed with Link's red necktie.

"Of course it's me." Taylor sniffled. "Who did you think it was?"

"S'rry, I'm a little sleepy. I meant, why're you all tied up?"

"Tell her *why* she's sleepy, Tay," Lindsey said. "Tell her why I tied you up."

"*You* tied her?"

Lindsey nodded proudly. "I came back from Miss Flora's office and found you catnapping. At least, I thought that's what was happening, until I saw a scratch magically start to form on your arm. And that's when I knew. . . ." She hitched her thumb at Taylor.

Sadie glanced down. Sure enough, there was a number 13 in the middle of her forearm. How had she not felt that? "What the heck, Taylor? This was you?"

First it was Lindsey in the middle of the night, then Amy in the woods, then Beak during the dance. She'd even scratched herself. *Herself!* How had Taylor managed to strike so many times without getting caught? "How? Why?"

Taylor began camouflaging to match Lindsey's black duvet cover.

"Oh, you turned invisible," Sadie said, feeling foolish. How had she not thought of that sooner? "Okay, then, *why*?"

"Everyone was taking too many risks," she began. "Wanting to be all loud and proud about our powers, sneaking out to the clearing, meeting up with boys, secret dances. . . . You were putting all of us in danger, and I didn't want to lose another friend, so I—"

"Tried to *kill* us?"

"I wasn't trying to kill you," Taylor said. "I was trying to scare you."

"Why didn't anyone feel the scratches? Why didn't anyone remember anything?"

"I swiped a few formulas from the Venom Chemistry lab. One for numbing skin, one to erase memory, and one for mild sedation."

"Mild?" Sadie screeched. "I can't move my arm, and Beak has been sleeping for days."

"I know. I suck at chemistry."

"Um, hello," Lindsey said. "The part I don't get is why you would scratch yourself. Was it so no one would suspect you?"

"Um, hi, *no*. It's because I needed some alone time. You guys were stressing me out."

"This is too weird." Lindsey began nibbling on her pinky nail.

"Don't bite," Sadie said. Then, "Why Beak?"

"You were acting all crushy around him, and I didn't want you to tell him we were lights."

"Crushy? I wasn't acting *crushy*!"

"Hey, Zendaya. Oh, hey, Frodo . . . ," Taylor said, mocking them.

"You were *there*?" Then, "Of course you were. That's how you knew about *cha-pee-leon*."

"Someone had to protect you."

"Irony alert!"

"Yeah, you were the one we needed protection *from,*" Lindsey said.

"Not true. I mean, okay, it's a little true, but the hunters who took Kate are still out there, and IBS still wants to experiment on us. That hasn't changed." Then her tone brightened. "Side note: you both looked super foxy. Sadie, you should wear skirts more often."

Lindsey looked to Sadie pleadingly. *What should we do*?

Sadie shrugged. What good would come from telling Miss Flora? The students were no longer in danger. But Taylor certainly would be if they turned her in.

Tears began falling from a face they couldn't see. "I'm really sorry. I didn't know what else to do."

"You could have asked me to stop," Lindsey said.

"I did. Like, ten thousand times."

"Solid point. My bad," Lindsey said, untying Taylor's arms. "You did shake things up around here. It was actually kind of fun."

"I'm sorry, too. Paws and claws?"

"Paws and claws," Lindsey said.

Taylor turned to Sadie. "Paws and claws?"

Sadie chose to pause instead.

If she had been watching this scene unfold in a movie, she'd definitely want her character to make up with Taylor. She'd root for their friendship and a happy ending. But this wasn't a movie; it was real life, and what Taylor had done was seriously messed up. At the same time, Sadie had put everyone in harm's way with Operation: STUD, and they'd forgiven her. So . . .

"At least there isn't some random maniac out there, so that's good," Sadie said. "But this is not over."

"What do you mean?" Taylor asked. "Are you going to tell on me?"

"If you do anything like this again, yes," Sadie said.

"I won't."

"Good. Because we're on a mission, and we don't need any more distractions."

"Mission?"

"While you were chilling in the infirmary, Amy was taken away for questioning, and we need to find her."

Taylor hissed. "Amy?"

"She's innocent, Tay," Lindsey said. "She didn't do this."

"How do you *know*?"

"Because *you* did."

"Solid point," Taylor said. "But she didn't save Kate. She just let her get taken."

"She was scared," Sadie said. "Anyway, we're forgiving you, so you have to forgive her."

"So that's it?" Taylor asked. "We're suddenly friends with Amy again?"

"If she forgives us."

"How are we supposed to make her forgive us?"

"By rescuing her from whatever Miss Flora locked her in," Lindsey said.

"Jail-dungeon? How do we do that? Our social hour is almost up."

"You're going to go into camo mode, search the school, and tell us where she is."

"By myself?"

"Yes, by yourself. Then during tomorrow's social hour, we'll go and apologize."

"It sounds way too dangerous," Taylor said. "Maybe we should text her instead."

"Miss Flora cut the Wi-Fi, remember? Besides, you kind of owe this to her, don'tcha think?"

Taylor cut a look to Lindsey. "Aren't *you* supposed to be making the rules?"

"Nah, I'm over it." Lindsey flopped onto her bed. "Being in charge is exhausting. From now on, it's all Sadie."

"All?" Sadie asked, hoping to have misunderstood Lindsey just a little. Because "all" meant all the glory, but it also meant all the epic fails, and that was a lot of responsibility for a girl who had absolutely no clue what she was doing.

"Yes, *all*," Lindsey purred. Then she added, "Good luck, lion. You're gonna need it."

twenty-two

"*This* is Miss Flora's jail-dungeon?" Lindsey hissed. "The old choir room?"

Taylor nodded. "It's the only door that's locked, so I figured Amy must be in here."

"*Figured?*" Sadie snipped. Because, come on, this was not the time for half-baked hunches. The chapel was on Sun, the floor above their rooms. If they were going to find Amy, they'd have to do it in the next thirty minutes. After that, social hour would be over, and the girls would be on lockdown for another night. And who knew what state Amy would be in after that.

"Did you try knocking?" Sadie pressed.

"Um, hello, yes."

"What about listening?"

"No point. The room's been soundproofed."

Tingles of fear prickled the back of Sadie's neck. How far was the headmistress willing to go for a confession? Far enough to make Amy scream? "Do you think Miss Flora's trying to cover up torture sounds?"

"No." Lindsey laughed. "The nuns did it so the choir could practice without the congregation hearing."

Relieved, Sadie leaned into the door and sniff-sniffed. A dank, earthy scent clung to the wood like a fond memory—one that the carpet's moldy must threatened to erase. Beneath it all lay a faint trace of oranges and clove. "Taylor's right. Amy's in there."

"What if she's all . . . like . . . bloody?" Taylor asked.

Lindsey pushed back the sleeves of her gold satin pajama top. "Then we'll bust her out and take her to the hospital."

Taylor began nervously twisting the spikes of her Mohawk. "Trigger alert!"

"You're triggered by hospitals?"

"No, Linds. I'm triggered when you talk about busting out. Why are you so obsessed with escaping?"

"Because that's how our story has to end."

"With us getting captured by IBS?"

"No, with us being free to live like Typicals," Lindsey said. "Don't you want to watch movies in theaters instead of dorm rooms? Shop at malls instead of on websites? Get professional manicures instead of DIYs? Hang out with boys somewhere other than in the woods?"

"Yeah, I guess," Taylor said, still twisting those spikes. "But that's not happening anytime soon."

"I know, but someday. And I'm trying to get us there as quickly as possible."

The thought of this story ending soon made Sadie's insides pretzel. Despite the curfews, the speciesist behavior, and the unsolved mysteries, this was the first time she'd played a main character, the first time she'd had any lines, the first time she'd had hope for a happily ever after.

Sadie pressed her ear against the wood but heard nothing. "Amy, are you in there?" she jiggled the door handle. "Can you hear us?"

"Shhhh," Taylor hissed, her Mohawk turning a mix of red, green, blue, and yellow—the colors in the pane of stained glass behind her. "We should probably get out of here."

"Yes!" Lindsey boomed. "I knew you'd agree with me eventually."

"I said, *get* out, not bust out."

Lindsey exhaled a gusty sigh, gathered her gold nail-file necklace, and wiggled it into the keyhole. After a few seconds of tinkering, the lock clicked open.

Expecting to find medieval torture devices and the molted skin of a well-meaning twelve-year-old, the girls clutched each other in fear. Palms sweating, they inched inside.

"Whoa," Lindsey said as the smell of oranges and clove rushed to greet them. "I know that smell. . . . It's . . . it's . . ."

"Incredible," Taylor muttered. "What happened in here? This place used to be so . . . gray."

Judging by Taylor's slack jaw and wide eyes, the plush

grass-green rug that covered the linoleum was a recent addition. Along with the heat lamps that loomed like palm trees over a blow-up pool that burbled with oil. There was a banquet table adorned with fruit baskets, colorful veggie platters, gourmet mac and cheese, hard-boiled eggs, Red Vines, and gooey chocolate chip cookies. And without Ms. Finkle's watchful eye, Amy was free to swallow everything whole—no chewing required. It was a serpent girl's paradise.

Not that Amy seemed the least bit concerned about Ms. Finkle, watchful eyes, or . . . *anything* as she napped on a white fleece chaise. She was wearing a satin sleep mask and noise-canceling headphones, her body wrapped in a terry-cloth robe, her feet in two pairs of fuzzy socks.

"So much for medieval torture devices," Sadie said as she lifted the satin blindfold.

Amy shot up, fangs bared, hair bun bobbing. "What the—?" It took a moment for her eyes to adjust to the light. "Sadie? What are you doing here?" Then, "Are you wearing Kate's choker?"

Sadie felt her neck, as if equally surprised. "I, uh—" She looked to Lindsey for words she failed to find.

"I gave it to her," Lindsey said flatly. "Sadie's a cat. Cats wear cat's claw. It's basic logic. Don't read into it. Do not dwell. Now, what's with the five-star resort? No one treats me like this when I get in trouble."

Amy cut a look to Sadie. "What are *they* doing here?"

"They wanted to tell you something." Sadie raised an eyebrow at Lindsey and Taylor. *"Right?"*

"Right," Lindsey managed. "Um, Amy, we weren't totally accurate about a few things, so let's forgive, forget, and start fresh. Cool?"

"Agreed," Taylor said.

Amy stared back at them blankly. "Weren't totally *accurate*?"

"You know, like, a few of the details were kinda off."

"*Kinda* off?"

"Fine, super off."

Amy stood and tightened the belt on her robe with an insistent tug. "Go on. . . ."

"Well, you obviously weren't the Scratcher, because that was Taylor, and—"

"Taylor? *Why?*"

"I tried to scare you guys into following the rules so you'd be safe. It's ironic. I know."

"And stupid," Lindsey added.

"No, *stupid* is you guys thinking I would get rid of Kate on purpose," Amy said. "The scratching was a straight-up villain move."

"About that . . . ," Lindsey began. "We're the only ones who know Taylor did it. So, one teensy favor? . . . Please don't tell anyone, or she'll get expelled."

"Wait." Amy began pacing across the green shag. "You want me to forgive you so I don't tell?"

"Not completely," Lindsey said. "We mostly want you to forgive us so we can be friends again."

"Yeah," Taylor said, eyes pooling. "Big-time."

"You have Sadie now. You don't need me."

"Yes, we do."

Amy padded over to the food table and popped a melon ball into her mouth. "What for?"

"You always calm me down when I want to pounce," Lindsey said.

"You have our backs," Taylor said. "Even when we don't have yours."

"And you bump into things to make us laugh."

"No," Amy said. "I bump into things because I don't wear my glasses."

"Whatever," Lindsey said. "It's funny, so don't stop."

"Thanks." Amy half smiled.

"So, do you forgive us?" Lindsey tried.

"I don't know," Amy said. "Did you actually apologize?" Lindsey nodded.

"Really? I didn't hear you."

"Fine. I apologize."

"What?" Amy cupped her ear. "You have *Polish eyes*?" Sadie bit her lip to keep from laughing.

"No! I apologize."

"You're a ball of fries?"

"No! I apol-o-gize."

"You and Paul are guys?"

"Stop!" Lindsey whined. "You know I'm terrible at this."

Amy shrugged. The snake was strong.

"Fine! I'm sorry."

"For what?"

"I'm sorry for not trusting you. I'm sorry for not believing you. And I'm sorry I stopped talking to you, because I've really missed you."

"I'm sorry for all of that, too," Taylor said. "And for the scratching part."

Lindsey pulled a bottle of black nail polish from the pocket of her satin pants and gave it a shake. "Ready for your stripes?"

Amy offered Lindsey her hand. "Ready." She stepped closer, closing the gap between them.

"Ew," Lindsey said, fanning the air. "What's that smell?"

"It isn't me," Amy said.

"Yes, it is! You smell like my elixir. Are you trying to get your memory back, too?"

"Not that I can remember," Amy joked.

"Then why . . ."

Amy opened the cooler by the snack table, indicating the vials of amber liquid inside. "It must be these. Now that I'm healthy again, I'm back to, well, being unhealthy,

I guess. You know, making too much venom. So I have to drain it."

"Actually," Sadie said, "I think it's the opposite. I think Miss Flora *wants* you to make venom."

"That doesn't make sense," Amy said. "Why would she want that?"

"I went to check on you while you were in the infirmary, and Miss Flora was there, freaking out because your venom was all dried up."

Amy adjusted her sloping hair bun. "I don't get it."

"That makes four of us," Lindsey said.

"Four?"

"Maybe. I have enough personality for two people."

Sadie grinned. "Amy, you're not here because Miss Flora thinks you're dangerous. You're here because she needs your venom, and you have to be healthy to make it."

"Why does she need it?" Taylor asked.

"I don't know, but I'm going to find out."

"How?"

"By busting out of here?" Lindsey bellowed.

Taylor chucked a Red Vine at her. "Too soon!"

"And I'm not busting out of anywhere," Amy said. "This place is egg-cellent!" She chucked a hard-boiled egg at Lindsey's neck. It landed with a smack that made all of them laugh.

"Tomat-oh no you didn't!" Lindsey called as she whipped a grape tomato at Amy's forehead.

While the girls hurled food at one another, Sadie became distracted by that familiar sound of rushing water. How did a single sound say so much? *Listen to the feelings . . .* it reminded her. *That's where the message is. . . .*

In this case, Sadie's feelings weren't saying anything. They were shouting, "Miss Flora is hiding something!" And the message? Well, that wasn't as loud. But the venom, she decided, was a good way to crank up the volume.

Without another word, Sadie reached into the cooler and began stuffing the pocket of her sweatshirt with vials. "Take the rest and hide them," she told the girls. "And don't tell anyone."

"Why?" Taylor asked, her body beginning to fade.

"Just trust me," Sadie insisted. "Paws and claws?"

"Paws and claws." Lindsey raised her hand. Her gold bangles clanged as they settled around her elbow. "I don't know what's happening, but I love it!"

"I don't know what's happening and I hate it," Taylor said, assuming the position.

"Ahem." Amy cleared her throat. "What about paws, claws, and . . . scales!"

"Ew. No," Lindsey said. "Scales aren't fierce. How about paws, claws, and fangs?"

"Too vampire-y," Amy countered.

"Paws, claws, and saws?" Sadie said. "You know, because you snore."

Amy blushed. "I don't snore!"

"How about paws, claws, and *denial*," Sadie teased, "because, yes, you do."

Amy jokingly gnashed her teeth.

"I know!" Sadie announced. "What about paws, claws, and *jaws*!"

"Yes, yes, and yes!" Amy beamed as she made a fang-like V with her fingers.

Warmth surged inside Sadie as the girls pressed their hands together and sealed their bond. After years of searching for her people, she had finally found them. Yes, they were part animal, but that was the *best* part. The part that the Chloes and Sierras of the world would never get to experience. The part that made them special.

"What are you going to do with the vials?" Amy asked.

"I'm going to trade them."

"For what?"

Sadie hurried for the door. "The truth."

twenty-three

Sadie knocked lightly on Miss Flora's office door. When there was no reply, she pounded. Then she pounded a little harder. The headmistress was definitely in there. Light was seeping through the crack under the door; papers were being shuffled.

"Miss Flora?" Sadie called, more as a warning than a request. According to Google, she was about to commit extortion, and in most jurisdictions, that was a criminal offense. But allowing this nefarious woman to take advantage of her friends would have been even more criminal, so she turned the knob and let herself in.

"Hello, Sadie," Miss Flora said with a stiff smile. "Social hour is almost over. Aren't you supposed to be in your room?"

"Yes, but . . ." Sadie paused.

Miss Flora removed her glasses and rubbed the corners of her eyes. "But what?"

"I was wondering if you have a lost and found?"

"What for?"

Hands shaking, Sadie pulled a vial of venom from her sweatshirt pocket. "I found this."

Miss Flora stood. "Where?"

"The chapel."

"Thank you, dear. I'll take it." She held out her hand and smiled a little too sweetly.

Sadie closed her fist around the vial. "Is this Amy's venom?"

"I'm . . . I'm not really sure what it is until I test it."

Miss Flora's heartbeat quickened. She was lying.

"This is Amy's, isn't it?"

"As I said, I'm not sure."

"Why do you need it?" Sadie asked, giving the headmistress one last chance to tell the truth.

"She makes too much." Miss Flora reached for the vial.

Sadie drew back her hand. "You're lying."

"Excuse me?"

"If you had Amy drain her venom because it was bad for her, why were you upset when she couldn't make any? Why do you need it now?"

Miss Flora began rounding her desk. "I don't need it, and I'm not lying."

"Another lie!" Sadie smashed the vial against the wood

floor. The glass shattered, and amber liquid spilled like a small-town gossip.

"What are you doing?"

Sadie pulled another vial from her pocket. "Why are you keeping Amy in the choir room? Why is Lindsey taking that elixir? How did you know Beak's real name was Brett?"

"Sadie, I have no idea what you're talking about," Miss Flora insisted, hazel eyes wide with panic. "Just please . . . give me the—"

Sadie smashed the second vial.

"Stop. I'm begging you."

"No, Miss Flora, I'm begging *you*."

"For what?"

"The truth," Sadie said. "And if you don't give it to me, I'll smash every vial in that cooler of yours. Because I have them all, and—fun fact—I love the sound of shattering glass. I also love Charm House, and if it ends up being another place full of secretive grown-ups and backstabbing mean girls, I'm going to smash more than a few vials of venom." The words shot from her mouth like electric sparks. But she wasn't roaring, and she wasn't knocking over desks. She was communicating like a person, not a wild animal. A very indignant, frustrated person, but a person nonetheless.

Miss Flora sat on the edge of her desk and sighed. "Fine, just stop breaking them," she pleaded, her hands pressed together in prayer.

"I'll stop spilling when you start spilling," Sadie said, wishing the girls had been there to hear her say that. Because, come on. That line was pure money. "Do we have ourselves a deal?"

With another sigh, Miss Flora locked her office door and turned on her white-noise machine. "Deal."

twenty-four

"**I** don't understand," Miss Flora asked over the buzz of her white-noise machine. "Why do you care so much about this venom?"

Sadie helped herself to a seat on the couch and then rested her legs on the coffee table. Was it disrespectful? Very. But people in power positions rarely concerned themselves with things like respect. And in that moment, Sadie was pure power. "I don't care about the venom," she said. "I care about what you're hiding. Charm House is supposed to keep girls like me safe. And your secrets are making me feel super un."

"Un?"

"Unsafe."

"Well," Miss Flora said, sitting beside her. "Just because you *feel* un doesn't mean you *are* un. Remember, dear, feelings aren't facts."

Sadie pulled another vial of venom from her pocket and dangled it over the floor.

"Please! You don't know what you're doing."

"I know what I saw, and I know what you've been telling Amy, and it doesn't add up. So give me the truth or I'll—"

"Stop!" Miss Flora shouted, fingers splayed. "What you're asking . . . It's . . . it's too much secret for a girl your age to keep."

"Try me," Sadie said, indicating the smashed glass and amber liquid pooling on the floor. "And don't bother lying. I'll hear it if you do."

Miss Flora stood. "There's a certain student at Charm House who needs protecting."

"Don't we all need protecting?"

"Yes. But she's in a great deal of danger. . . ."

Kate, Sadie thought. It had to be.

"She also happens to be Professor Jo's daughter," Miss Flora continued. "And my granddaughter."

"Wait, so Professor Jo is your—"

"My daughter, yes. A glorious eagle light. Like you, she transferred to Charm House in the sixth grade. Only *she* worked tirelessly to control her instincts and graduated number one in her class. Because of her diligence, she got a wonderful job as a psychology professor at the University of Oregon, where she worked alongside Typicals until . . ." Miss Flora stopped herself and looked deep into Sadie's eyes. It was a chilly ocean breeze kind of look; it permeated Sadie's bones and turned her insides to ice.

"Until *what*?"

"Until her ten-year-old angel of a daughter became . . . unmanageable. She'd have wild bursts of aggression and extreme bossiness, followed by long bouts of isolation and restlessness. Her father, Karl, a Typical, who also happens to be the medical director at IBS and an unfit husband, wanted to subject her to a battery of invasive tests."

Sadie stiffened. "The Thirteenth Floor?"

"No, he hadn't invented that yet. But he insisted they admit her to the institute." Miss Flora deepened her voice to something more manly. "What will people say if they find out a renowned psychologist has a crazy kid he couldn't fix?" She shuddered at the memory. "But Jo knew her daughter was a light. She knew there was no fixing her."

"So they're working on a cure that will never exist?"

"It doesn't exist yet. But hopefully one day," Miss Flora said, as if dimming the lights was her goal.

There was a time not too long before when Sadie would have shared that goal. A time when finding a "cure" for her light was all she wanted. But now, not so much. The leonine traits that made her an outcast were now her biggest source of pride: the strength that allowed her to carry her sick friend through the woods, her keen sense of smell, her record-breaking speed, her lie-detecting hearing, her ability to pull all-nighters . . . If IBS found a cure, those gifts would be gone.

"So Jo filed for a divorce, which was long overdue, in my

opinion," Miss Flora continued. "And Karl, who was married to his work, barely flinched. She told him she was taking the kids to the East Coast. Instead, they came here."

Sadie held her breath and listened for Miss Flora's heartbeat. It was calm and steady. She was telling the truth. "It's Kate, isn't it?"

"Kate?"

"Your granddaughter. Karl found her and took her to IBS, didn't he?"

Miss Flora turned to face the window—the one that had been streaked with rain on Sadie's first day. Now all she saw was a clear night sky studded with twinkling stars.

"That's enough for today."

"It has to be Kate," Sadie contended. "No one has ever referred to Professor Jo as Mom since I've been here, so who else could it—"

"I said, that's enough!"

Sadie folded her hands behind her head and lifted her gaze to the iron candelabra. *Ahhh, the power.* "Kate it is."

"It's not Kate."

"Then why hasn't anyone ever mentioned Professor Jo's daughter before?"

"Because no one knows about her," Miss Flora finally admitted. "Not even the daughter."

Sadie twisted her coarse hair around her finger. How

was that even possible? Unless . . . There was one girl at Charm House who didn't know who her parents were. One girl whose memory had mysteriously failed her. One girl who was able to finish Professor Jo's sentence in class when no one else could. . . .

"Lindsey?"

Miss Flora nodded slowly, her head heavy with shame, or guilt, whatever it is that makes adults behave the way they do.

"You have to tell her! She has no idea who her parents are. She thinks she lost her memory!"

Miss Flora turned; her expression, once vulnerable, was now hard and grave. "Yes, and we must keep it that way."

"Why?"

"Because Lindsey is desperate for real life but doesn't have the self-control to handle it. One roar, one fight, one show of strength, and she'd be on a watch list. The same watch list that lands on her father's desk every day." Miss Flora closed her eyes and let out a steadying breath. "The only thing keeping her here, keeping her safe, is that she wouldn't know where to go if she got out. And she needs to keep believing that. Do you understand?"

"Not really." Sadie buried her face in a throw pillow, as if its fibers could absorb her confusion. "Why doesn't she recognize her own mother? Why can't she recognize you?"

Miss Flora pointed at the amber-colored puddle on the floor. "Three teaspoons of venom, along with daily hypnosis, makes Lindsey forget her past. When Amy was sick, the venom lost its potency. That's why Lindsey got those headaches. It's also why she started to remember. And I need that venom to make her forget."

Sadie had been right: the reason Amy was living la vida loca in the choir room was to keep her healthy so she'd make more venom. "What about Beak? Why did Lindsey's head hurt when she saw him?"

"Brett is my grandson."

"Lindsey's *brother*?" It certainly explained why he and Lindsey malfunctioned when they saw each other in the woods. They were siblings, and somewhere in the crevices of her mind she must have known it.

"But Lindsey's last name is Striker, and his is Van der Beak?"

"We changed her name because of the—"

"Lie."

"It's not a lie, Sadie. It's the only way we know how to keep her safe. How to keep all of you safe."

"What about Brett? Is he a light, too?" Sadie smiled a little. He certainly was to her.

"No, he's a Typical, along with the other boys at Allendale. But that's about the only thing they have in common. He's too sensitive for those towel-snapping jocks. We only sent him there to keep him close."

"Is he okay?"

Miss Flora held her hands together in gratitude. "He went back to school yesterday, thanks to Nurse Walker."

Sadie was mostly relieved, but part of her liked knowing that she and Beak were under the same roof. She liked the possibility of being able to run into him at any moment. Now that he was gone, would she ever see him again? "Does he know about . . ."

"Yes, but he'd never tell. He knows what's at stake." Miss Flora put her hands in the pockets of her slacks. "So, I answered all your questions. Now you answer mine."

Sadie sat up. A quid pro quo was not part of her plan.

"Where are you keeping the rest of Amy's venom? Lindsey will need another dose in the morning."

"I'll bring it to you once you meet my terms."

Miss Flora stiffened. "Terms?"

Sadie's insides soared. Making the rules was exhilarating. "I have two more things. Thing one: Everyone thinks Amy was the Scratcher, but she wasn't. So if you could let everybody know that it was someone from IBS and that they've been arrested, that would be great."

Miss Flora drew back her head "I'm not going to *lie*."

"Um, it's a little late for that."

"Sadie, if the person is still out there—"

"It's safe. I promise. I know who did it, and it will never happen again. Thing two: let us have the dance back."

"Absolutely not. Brett called his mother during your last

dance and told her how brazen you girls were acting. You're far from ready."

"What if we put in extra hours with Professor Jo? A full weekend of Instinct Control. No, a full week!" Sadie tried. "When it's over, we'll be even more boring than the Typicals. I promise."

"The only promise I want you to make, dear, is that you will keep everything I told you to yourself."

"Only if you let us have the dance."

A low-pitched grumble began building inside the headmistress's throat. It could easily have been mistaken for a hunger pang, but her knit brows and narrowed eyes suggested something far worse than low blood sugar.

"Miss Flora?" Sadie peeped, spooked by the sudden change in her demeanor. "Is everything—"

"PROMISE ME!" she roared. The papers on her desk blew to the floor. The candelabra shook. Its tiny flames flickered.

Sadie's pulse hammered.

"PROMISE ME!"

"Promise," she mouthed, her throat too dry to speak.

Miss Flora's lips curled into a Cheshire cat smile. The kind a lioness makes once she's trapped her prey. "Whose heart is beating now?" She began pacing, eyes fierce and fixed on Sadie; pinning her to the couch with the intensity of her ire.

Trembling, Sadie wondered if it was possible to barf lungs. Her insides were that desperate to escape. Her outsides, too.

"There's always a bigger cat, Miss Samson," the headmistress growled. "Keep that pride of yours in check, or next time this cat just might get your tongue. Now bring me the rest of that venom, and tell your friend Taylor that if she so much as scratches a mosquito bite, I'll send her to the Thirteenth Floor myself."

"You knew?"

"There's always a bigger cat," she repeated.

Sadie didn't dare ask how Miss Flora knew about Taylor, and she double didn't dare press the dance issue. Every instinct in her body told her to stuff her proverbial tail between her legs and do what she was told.

twenty-five

"*I* need the venom!" Sadie cried as she burst into Lindsey and Taylor's room. Her insides were still quaking from Miss Flora's roar, her thoughts still knotted from the shock of it all. "Hurry!"

Lindsey was seated on the pink rug painting fresh black stripes down Amy's fingernails. Taylor was kneeling behind them, flat-ironing Amy's hair.

"Wait. I thought you were staying in the choir room tonight," Sadie said.

"We busted her out!" Lindsey said proudly. Then, "Ew, Sadie Lady. Are you okay? Your skin is very Don't Pretzel My Buttons."

"What's that?"

Lindsey held up a bottle of OPI nail polish, its color a sickly beige.

"I'm fine," Sadie asserted. "I just need the venom."

Lindsey flicked her chin toward the closet. "Behind the shoebox tower."

"Did you figure out what Miss Flora is doing with it?" Amy asked.

"Turns out your venom is . . . special."

Amy beamed. "Special *how*?"

"Uh, it's some kind of magic medicine," Sadie reported from inside the closet. "It cures, like, hundreds of things. Nurse Walker uses it all the time, and she's running out, so . . ." Sadie moved the shoeboxes aside while thanking her lucky stars that Lindsey didn't know about her own people's built-in lie detector. If she had known, she would have heard Sadie's heart woodpeckering against her chest. "Got it!"

"I can't believe my venom is magic," Amy said, sitting up a little taller. "Does Miss Flora think I have other powers? What else did she say about me?"

"Just that she needs the venom back right away."

With that, Sadie grabbed the cooler and bolted before they asked another question she was not allowed to answer.

The following morning, the Charm House girls woke to an announcement from Miss Flora. "Great news, students," she began. "Thanks to the hard work of our dedicated staff, we have found the prankster responsible for the scratching incidents. As a result, the shelter-in-place protocols have been lifted. You're free to resume your normal activities and class schedules. We can assure you that nothing like that will ever happen again."

A chorus of sleepy but relieved hisses echoed through the hallways.

"In other news," the headmistress continued, "Professor Jo has a very special opportunity for those of you interested in mastering the art of instinct control. It's an intense seven-day clinic designed to teach you how to override your instincts so you can blend in with Typicals. At the end of the seven days, there will be an exam. Those who pass can attend a dance with the Allendale boys. Those who don't will be on the cleanup committee. The course sign-up sheet will be circulated at breakfast."

The hallway hisses grew louder as the girls celebrated this unexpected turn of events. They chanted in praise of Miss Flora. They chanted in praise of Professor Jo. They even chanted in praise of the Allendale boys, who had zero to do with anything. Sadie, however, could barely bring herself to smile.

The intense seven-day clinic had been her idea, and Miss Flora was giving Professor Jo all the credit. But after a quick visit to the Den to vent her frustrations, the Whisper told her to get used to it. "Great leaders take all the blame and none of the credit," she explained.

"Nothing about that sounds *great* to me," Sadie responded.

Still, she got the point and kept her resentful mouth shut,

knowing that there was a bright side to her sacrifice: if she worked like mad to pass Professor Jo's exam, she'd finally get that dance with Beak.

But after the first two days of training, Sadie and the other girls began to wonder if passing was even an option. Role-playing exercises called "An Allendale Boy Gets Handsy," "You're Crushing and He's Not," "He's Crushing and You're Not," "She Just Cut the Bathroom Line," and "To Kiss or Not to Kiss" had pushed them to the breaking point. Throughout the week, tedious lectures on coping with feeling shy, embarrassed, hungry, jealous, elated, or madly in love had tested their attention spans more than anything else. And a series of early-morning obstacle courses called "Senses That Make Sense" had presented them with physical challenges but prohibited them from using their animal abilities to overcome them. So instead of moving boulders aside, scaling trees for safety, or contorting their bodies to make narrow escapes, they had to know where a Typical would tap out and quit. It had been a grueling week, but with the dance as their reward, everyone had managed to push through and pass.

Now, with only one sleep left before the dance, Lindsey was sorting through her overflowing closet, helping the girls finalize their outfits. "Too on the nose?" she said, holding a tiger-striped body-con dress against her torso. Then something struck her. "Hey, Sadie Lady, remember when you said the jungle theme was too much like our lives?"

"Yeah, why?" Sadie asked, remembering their walk in the woods three weeks earlier and thinking about how much their relationship had changed since then. It was no longer based on Lindsey's need for protection or Sadie's desperation for friends. It was about mutual respect. Well, mostly mutual. Lindsey was tired of being in charge, while Sadie was getting more and more comfortable in the role. Decisions were becoming like Starburst candies: when one was gone, she craved another.

"What if we change things up a little?" Lindsey said.

"I don't like where this is going," Taylor said.

"Same," Amy said. "We spent all week decorating the gym. It's too late for changes."

"They're right," Sadie said. "This theme cannot be un-themed. There's no time."

It had taken days to cover the gym walls in leaves, hours to carpet the floor with Astroturf, and an entire afternoon to hang the green twinkle lights and blue tulle that cascaded from the bleachers like waterfalls. Not only was it too late for changes, it was unnecessary. The setting was magical.

"Um, hello. Obviously," Lindsey said. "I don't want to change the *decorations*. I want to change *us*."

The following night, when the Pack arrived at the dance (forty minutes late, to make an entrance), they supermod-eled onto the scene dressed as each other's lights. Taylor wore Lindsey's tiger-print dress with brown suede booties. Amy wore a savanna-tan romper, her hair teased wildly around her face like Sadie's mane. Lindsey rocked Amy's snakeskin minidress with black sneakers and Link's red tie knotted loosely around her waist. And Sadie dazzled in a shimmery, iridescent maxi-dress that shifted from pink to blue to purple to green, depending on how the light hit it. It was the closest thing to camouflage she could find. It was also big-time ironic, since Sadie had never felt more seen in her life.

As "Welcome to the Jungle" by Guns N' Roses blasted through the gym, girls with sweat-soaked bangs and breathless boys complimented the Pack on the "sick" decorations, the "epic" playlist, and their "superhot" outfits. Beak, however, was not one of them. Was he still recovering? Too afraid to see Lindsey? What if he was crushing on a Typical girl and wanted nothing to do with his sister's weirdo friends?

The song changed to "Say So" by Doja Cat, and Val, Mia, and Liv began knocking out some major @charlidamelio choreography while everyone cheered them on. Well, everyone except Lindsey, whose claws came out as she watched the hyenas soak up attention that should have been hers.

"Would anyone care to join me on the dance floor?" she asked through gritted teeth. She was trying to control her competitive instincts the way Professor Jo had trained them to.

"That sounds exciting and fun," Taylor said, also mocking their lessons.

"It certainly does, Taylor. Count me in," Amy added,

playing along. "Sadie, are you interested in moving your body to some pop music beats?"

"Thank you for asking, Amy. I'd love to move my body to pop music—"

"Hey, Zendaya."

Sadie spun around to find Beak, the only boy at the dance not wearing a wrinkled T-shirt and saggy jeans. His denim was dark and fitted, his shirt crisp, sleeves rolled. His black hair was slicked, and his green eyes were distracting. He wasn't awkward or squirmy, like so many of the other boys. He didn't round his shoulders or shift nervously from one foot to the other. He was self-assured and present. The kind of boy who writes songs about crushes and isn't afraid to sing them.

"Can I talk to you for a second?"

Sadie's cheeks grew hot. "What about?" she asked, like a confident girl might.

Beak tilted his head, inviting her to step away from her friends so they could have a moment of privacy. Sadie stepped, but nervous giggles and curious stares followed her anyway.

"I wanted to thank you," he said once they were alone.

"Oh." Sadie managed to grin, even though she was a bit disappointed. She would have preferred a marriage proposal. "Thank me for what?"

"Are you serious?"

"Oh, you mean that time I carried you through the woods while you were delirious and fighting for your life?"

"Yeah," he snickered. *"That."*

Sadie smiled. "No problem. You were super light."

Beak laughed. Sadie's insides tingled with the dancing mist. Then . . . nothing.

Awkward silence filled the space between them. And to make things worse, the Pack was dancing around them, trying to appear like three girls *not* eavesdropping or spying, which they absolutely were. So now what? Was Beak going to ask her to dance? Was she supposed to ask him? Did he think her dress was too shiny? Not shiny enough? Did he think the word *shiny* sounded all nasally when it was said too much?

"So, I have a question," Beak finally said.

"Does it have to do with the word *shiny*?"

"Uh, no. It has to do with you."

Sadie's face got hot all over again. "What about me?"

"Do you want to dance?"

"Depends," she said, grateful to be back in the power position.

"On what?"

"On how many questions *I* get."

Beak half smiled, a fetching movie star wondering if he'd met his match. "How many questions do you want?"

"Two."

The song changed to "Without Me" by Halsey. He took her hand and led her onto the dance floor. "Granted."

It was impossible to know if the Pack was still watching them. Every sight, sound, and smell around Sadie disintegrated into glitter-colored dust and drifted away. All she saw and heard and smelled was Beak.

"Sooo . . . ," he said as they found the slow beat of the song and swayed.

"So, *what*?" Sadie asked, wondering if her hair was tickling his nostrils or scratching the bottom of his chin.

"Your question?"

"Oh, yeah, right. So, um, where did you get that scar on your cheek?" she asked, distracted by the heat of his palms, imagining two handprints burned onto her waist.

"I was at a coffee shop with my sister after school one day, and she cut the line. The girl in front of her said, 'Excuse me, but I was here first,' and my sister flipped out. I pulled her away from the girl and got clawed."

"Whoa," Sadie said, all too aware of Lindsey's strength. "Good thing you were there to step in."

"Yeah, it started happening a lot, and I always seemed to be there when it did. Which was good, I guess. But I always worried about *not* being there, you know? Like what would happen if she freaked out and I wasn't around to save everyone?"

"The whole brass-ring thing," Sadie said, remembering Beak's mention of Phoebe from *The Catcher in the Rye*. How

195

Holden realized that he wasn't always going to be around to protect his sister—that she'd eventually have to face the consequences of her actions. That there was nothing he could do about it.

Beak nodded. "The next day she ran off and joined the circus. I haven't seen her in five years. Which is fine. I hate the circus."

Sadie's insides sank. She didn't need to hear Beak's speeding heart to know that his story was fake. Lindsey was right there, dancing six feet away from them. Disappointed, Sadie wiggled from his grip.

"I'm kidding!" he said, pulling her back. "I know you know the truth. My grandmother told me."

The mist returned. Mostly because of his honesty, but also because he was breathing against her neck the way he had when she'd carried him through the woods. Only this time it wasn't an accident; he was that close on purpose.

"At first I couldn't believe she trusted you with all of this," Beak admitted. "Not because it's you, but because it's anyone. My mom tried so hard to keep it from my dad, it just seemed . . ."

"Risky?"

"Yeah, risky. But now I'm glad you know. It was a lot to keep to myself."

"I get it." Sadie thought of her friends, their honesty pact, and all the lies she'd had to tell them, all the lies she'd have to keep telling them, in order to guard the secret.

"So, what's your second question?" Beak asked, lightening the mood.

Their eyes locked. It felt like looking straight into the sun. "When we met, you were hiding something behind your back. What was it?"

He looked past her shoulder, stalling. "It's embarrassing."

"Embarrassing? Really? Have you seen my—" She pointed at her mane.

"Your hair is not embarrassing," he said. "It's your signature feature—like Billie Eilish's bored face or the Rock's biceps. Every cool person has an SF. Except me. I have three."

Sadie giggled. "And they are . . . ?"

"My beak-like nose, my C-shaped scar, and my personality."

"Is that personality going to answer my question?"

"What was it again?"

"What were you hiding behind your back?"

Beak sighed. *"It's Kind of a Funny Story."*

"I'm listening."

He chuckled. "No, that's the name of a book. *It's Kind of a Funny Story,* by Ned Vizzini."

"You were hiding a *book*? Why?"

"Every time one of these Allendale jockstraps catches me

reading, I get called Beakworm, which is a really tragic play on *bookworm,* and I'm over it. So, during my free time I hide in the woods and read."

Sadie wanted to hug him. She wanted to tell him that she liked the *Glee* soundtrack covers better than the originals, that she cried when old people held hands, and that she loved dipping popcorn in hummus. She wanted to tell him Chloe and Sienna called her Hairy Poppins and that they'd write Sa-DIE on her locker. That she hadn't had friends until she came to Charm House and that she wanted to dance with him forever. But she controlled her instincts and simply said, "Reading is cool."

Was it fair to demand the truth from others but not from herself? No. But nature wasn't about fairness; it was about survival. And Sadie Samson was determined to survive. Her jungle, her rules.

Starting now.

Acknowledgments

Many people assume authors are solitary creatures, and they aren't wrong. I spend most days alone. When I have to go out, I enjoy talking to myself under the protective cover of my PPE mask. And when I'm interrupted midthought, I am mildly—okay, severely irritated. So yes, I am a lone wolf. That said, I have another kind of PPE that helps me survive. Instead of personal protective equipment, this PPE stands for Publishing Pack Extraordinaire. Without the geniuses in this pack, the novel you are holding/listening to would not exist.

Kelsey Horton, editor extraordinaire, is my alpha. Talk about instincts. Her guidance and faith in me were fierce, and I couldn't be more grateful. Global pandemics have a way of messing with a girl's head. Schedules were off, creativity was compromised, and hope was waning. Had it not been for Kelsey's unwavering patience, understanding, and support, you'd be holding a book with a wildly cute cover, filled with a lot of blank pages.

I owe one billion thank-yous to Barbara Marcus, president

of the children's division at Random House. And another one billion thank-yous to the publisher, Beverly Horowitz. You are next-level alphas and real inspirations.

Carol Ly and team are responsible for the book's aforementioned wildly cute cover. Catherine O'Mara and her marketing pack, along with Emma Benshoff and her publicity pack, are the reasons you know it exists.

If you assumed I'm a spelling and grammar wiz, well, you be wrong. Copyeditors Barbara Bakowski and Colleen Fellingham scrutinized this manuscript to make sure you never had to read sentences that ended with "you be wronge."

My personal pack of beasts includes Richard Abate, my badass agent of eighteen years—FUMP; Martha Stevens, his fabulous assistant, who always converts meeting times to PST so I don't show up three hours late; James Gregorio, my unflappable lawyer; Zara Lisbon who provides daily assistance; and the middle school girls in my Laguna Beach Clique Club, who inspire me every day (My two wonderful sons, Luke and Jesse, find me painfully embarrassing. Thank you, girls, for making believe I'm still kinda cool).

As always, Mom, Dad, Best Sis, and Knuckles: thanks to your bottomless love, this lone wolf has never been truly alone.

XOXO Lisi

The Pack seems stronger than ever—but Sadie has a secret that could claw its way out.

**TURN THE PAGE FOR A PREVIEW
OF BOOK TWO IN THE PACK SERIES.**

one

The classroom smelled like a Sephora. Instead of paying attention to Professor Norma's snoozer of a lecture on landforms, the caged animal-lights were swiping fruit-flavored gloss across their lips and rubbing floral-scented salves into their hands—all in anticipation of that final gong. Once struck, Typical Topics would be over, and the most anticipated weekend of the year (since last month's dance with the Allendale boys) would finally begin.

Sadie gazed beyond the metal-framed windows. Those smoke-gray clouds were still hovering. Oppressive and suffocating, they loomed above the private grounds of the Charm House boarding school like an overbearing parent, there to put a damper on her plans and, even worse, her new hairstyle. Hair that Sadie spent most of the day admiring in the reflection of her dead laptop screen.

She'd meant to charge her computer the night before. Really. But Claw Spa, the new beauty salon Sadie was opening with her pack mates, had become a major attention suck.

Saturday morning was fully booked, and they were wildly unprepared.

Lindsey, tiger-light and queen of the claws, had to set up a manicure table. Taylor, chameleon-light and color expert, needed a dyeing station. Amy, snake-light and scaly skin specialist, had to blend her oil treatments. And Sadie, lion-light with superhuman strength and a dry blond mane, was stuck rearranging furniture—a bummer, but not a surprise.

They had finished setting up around midnight. While Lindsey, Taylor, and Amy applauded their work, Sadie, now surrounded by mirrors, fixated on her unruly hair. Gathering it in a bristly bundle, she tried twisting it into something elegant at the nape of her neck. Tying straw into a bow would have been easier. "I should just shave it off."

"Funny," Taylor said as she worked her short pink layers into spikes. "I've been thinking about all of that"—she waved her hand in the general vicinity of Sadie's head—"and I have an idea. Trust me."

"You've been *thinking* about it?" How long had Taylor been contemplating Sadie's look? "Is it *that* bad?" Her stomach dipped as she remembered the girls at her old school, how they called her Hairy Poppins. And Taylor's whole "trust me" thing? That was an elephant-sized ask.

Only weeks earlier, Taylor had secretly terrorized the animal-lights—and worse, her own pack mates. Her plan was to scare the girls (mostly Lindsey) so they would stop sneaking out to meet the boys. If the animal-lights were discovered, the evil doctors at Institute of Behavioral Science would lock them in cages on the thirteenth floor, just like they did with Kate, and experiment on them 24/7. So Taylor's intention was to keep them safe. *But really, T? Did you have to turn invisible, scratch venom into our bodies to make us sleep, then carve the number 13 into our skin? You couldn't think of any other way to keep us safe from IBS? Nothing?*

Apparently, she couldn't. And technically, that was fine. Taylor meant well and the Pack forgave her. But "trust"? Yeah, that was going to take a while.

"Sadie, I'm not saying your frizzy vibe is *brutal*," she continued. "I'm just—"

"Then I'll say it," Lindsey interrupted, her emerald-green eyes fierce and focused. "Sadie Lady, we love you, but your frizzy vibe is brutal."

"*Brutal* is a little harsh," Amy said. "*Brittle* is more appropriate." Her sympathetic smile revealed one fang on either side of her mouth. "Why don't I heat some orange and clove oil and—"

"We can give you a mane-over!" Taylor bellowed.

"Purrrfect," Lindsey said. "I'll do her claws!"

Two hours later, Sadie was running the sharp points of her gold nails through flat-ironed, deep-conditioned blond hair that faded to black.

"Wow, you look sixteen!" Amy gushed.

"Yeah, the ombré technique is a total mane-changer," Taylor said. "And the dark tips hide your split ends."

"You actually look pretty!" Lindsey added.

"Actually?"

"Not that you didn't look pretty before. You did. On the inside. But now you're pretty on the outside, too."

Sadie was too excited about her mane-over to be offended. Before heading to bed, Taylor gave her a bottle of dry shampoo and strict instructions not to get her hair wet or it would frizz again. Which was why Sadie was currently admiring her reflection in a dead laptop screen and praying the rain away instead of listening to—

"Miss Samson!" Professor Norma shouted, or maybe it just sounded like a shout because of Sadie's extra-sensitive hearing. "Are you paying attention?"

Chairs creaked as everyone turned.

"Uh . . ." Sadie's cheeks warmed. "You were talking about animal migration."

"Correct. I *was* talking about animal migration. Twenty minutes ago . . ."

The hyena-lights giggled. Jealous of the Pack's popularity, they feasted on their misfortunes.

"Now I'm asking our Charm Club leaders for status reports, and since you're one of those leaders, why don't you update us on your progress."

Lindsey, Taylor, and Amy glared at Sadie, silently reminding her not to divulge their secret. As if she needed a reminder. The Charm Club project was worth 50 percent of their Typical Topics grade. And with her slipping GPA, Sadie was counting on a high score to bring up her average. If word got out that their club, the Claw Spa, was charging for treatments, they'd fail. Granted, the Pack wasn't asking for money. Just that customers cover the Pack's chores and hand over their desserts whenever asked. This seemed like a reasonable request, considering Claw Spa was the only club providing an essential service. But try telling that to a professor preaching a free-flowing exchange of ideas and teamwork.

"Our progress?" Sadie lowered the screen on her laptop. "Um, last night we set up the spa in our dorm rooms, and it opens tomorrow. That's about it."

Professor Norma lowered her glasses, which were attached to a beaded string that held them around her neck, against her navy cardigan. Her small features were tight, and her makeup-free skin was the color of Silly Putty. She was probably a terrible joke-teller. "Can you share your most positive experience so far?"

Sadie reached for the glossy tips of her hair and sat up a little taller. "Um, the Allendale football game is tomorrow night, and Family Day is Sunday, so we're booked solid, which is cool."

"Sounds promising." The professor searched Sadie's eyes like hiding places. "And your most challenging experience?"

"Fitting everyone in, I guess. Demand is pretty high."

"Well, you are offering a *free* service."

"Free?" Val yipped. "Ha!" She and the other hyena-lights had started a comedy club named Cackle. Ever since Professor Norma had said she thought the name was clever (*cackle* is the sound of a laugh, and it's also the name for a group of hyenas), Val had been incredibly cocky.

Professor Norma folded her arms across her dangling glasses. "Is there a problem?"

"Only if you think doing someone else's chores is a—"

Lindsey growled softly.

"Chores?" Professor Norma's thin eyebrows arched.

Lindsey glowered at Val and whispered, "Watch it, hy-e-nerd," knowing that Professor Norma couldn't hear her.

"Val, are you suggesting that—"

"Nope. All good. I was just workshopping one of my jokes for the Family Day showcase. I guess it needs more work. Sorry about that."

Unlike the other teachers at Charm House, Professor "Normal" did not have an animal-light, so quiet whispers often went undetected. Sadie often wondered why Headmistress Flora had hired a Typical in the first place. Yes, she taught Typical Topics, so that part made sense, but still. The whole point of Charm House was to protect its students from the outside world. A world in which researchers from the Institute of Behavioral Science hunted animal-lights and imprisoned them on the thirteenth floor of their creepy building, where they experimented on their prisoners and would continue to do so until the source of their animal powers was uncovered. Professor Norma's daughter was a light, which was why everyone trusted her. But what kind of light? And where was this daughter? Was she with Kate—Amy's old roommate, who had been captured by IBS the week before Sadie arrived? No one seemed to know.

"Who else will be presenting their club during the Family Day showcase?" the professor asked.

Before anyone could answer, the gong rang. The weekend had officially started, and the students began clearing out.

"Miss Samson, may I have a few words?"

"Of course." Smiling, Sadie made her way to the front of the room, anticipating another compliment. All her other teachers had had something positive to say about her hair, and every student (except the hyena-lights, of course) had booked a spa appointment, hoping for a similar look. If Professor Normal's few words were flattering, she could have as many as she wanted.

"I've noticed a change in you lately," she said once Sadie approached her desk.

"I elevated my style."

Professor Normal glimpsed at Sadie's black tips. "I see that."

An awkward silence filled the space between them. A

space that no longer smelled like fruity gloss and floral salves. Just tension.

"Any chance of you elevating your grades?"

"My *grades*?" Was *that* was this was about? Because come on. For the first time, Sadie had best friends, regular friends, and a crush on an Allendale boy who liked her back. As the only lion-light at Charm House, she no longer feared mean girls; they feared *her*. She was CEO of Claw Spa. Boss-lady of the jungle. Leader of the Pack. Yes, socializing had been cutting into her study time lately. But she'd bounce back. Good grades had always come easy to her. But BFFs? Not as much.

"I'm concerned," Professor Normal said with a coffee-scented sigh. "The other teachers are, too."

"Don't worry. I'm a cat. We always land on our feet."

"Do you think your parents will feel the same way?"

"I do," Sadie said, sure of it. Her parents always wanted her to branch out and make friends. So yeah, they would feel the same way. How could they not?

two

*T*he Claw Spa opened its dorm-room doors immediately after breakfast, and now Sadie's bacon-free belly was shouting, *Time for lunch!* Had it been five hours already? She chased her hunger with cucumber-infused water, then greeted her next customer.

"Welcome to Claw Spa," she said to Sondra, a petite rat-light with chin zits and oily brown hair. "Checking in?"

Sondra nodded, brows raised, smile wide. Like a caterpillar on the verge of metamorphosis, she, and the dozens who checked in before her, wanted a beauty transformation, just like Sadie's. "I'm getting ombré hair with Taylor and an oil treatment with Amy."

"Same," said her friend Kara—a dingo-light with deep-set brown eyes and sharp, uneven teeth. "Can you see if Lindsey has time to do my nails?"

Sadie checked her spreadsheet. "I can squeeze you in with Lindsey if Sondra skips her treatment with Amy."

Did it make sense? No. Amy's schedule had nothing to do

with Lindsey's. But someone had to stop Sondra from getting an oil treatment, or her already greasy hair would look wet.

"What do you say?" Sadie asked, desperate to speed things up. The check-in line was snaking into the hallway, and the reception area was standing room only. The beds, which Sadie converted into couches thanks to some creative pillow placement, were taken. Same with the four chairs she positioned under Amy's heat lamp. Who knew the hot orange light, meant for warming cold-blooded reptiles, could cut nail-polish drying time in half? Lindsey, that's who.

Sondra approved the change, and Kara thanked her with a suffocating hug.

"Once you agree to the terms, you'll be all set." Sadie folded a piece of paper and slid it across her desk. It read: *Kara and Sondra do our laundry Monday, November 8.* Then she handed them a pen. "Your signatures, please."

They scribbled their names without hesitation, and Sadie filed the paper away in her desk drawer. "Next!"

Rachel stepped forward. An energetic monkey-light with a nasty nail-biting habit and the swollen cuticles to prove it. "One manicure, please."

"What about a hot oil hand massage?" Sadie said, realizing that Sondra's cancellation left Amy wide open. "Those cuticles look parched." If Rachel's bloody nubs came within five feet of Lindsey, she'd pack up her Caboodles kit and walk off the job.

"But I booked a manicure."

"Yeah, but right now, you need a little less mani and a lot more *cure*. The oil treatment will be perfect."

Rachel began nibbling on her thumbnail.

"Trust me." Sadie slid a folded piece of paper across her desk, which Rachel promptly signed. Now that Sadie had someone to return the water glasses to the cafeteria after closing, she could dry-shampoo her hair, raid Lindsey's closet for a flattering outfit, and get to Allendale without missing a second of the football game.

Not that Sadie liked football. She loathed it. Her father, a San Francisco superfan, always shouted at the TV when the 49ers played. Which, thanks to Sadie's super-sensitive lion-light hearing, sounded like he was screaming into a megaphone aimed at a microphone.

It was Beak she looked forward to—a like-minded sports hater who also preferred books to balls. And she hadn't seen him, or his distracting green eyes, since the dance, four weeks earlier. She listened to "Without Me" by Halsey several times a day to relive their magical night.

Beak's warm breath against her neck while they swayed to the heart-pounding beat of the song. The grape bubble gum scent of his skin. How the twinkle lights in the gym hinted at the C-shaped scar on his cheek—a scar he got while breaking up a fight between his sister and an innocent girl at a coffee shop. How he shared his most guarded secret—that this sister was Lindsey—and Lindsey had no idea that Beak was her brother. . . .

Granted, Beak already knew that Miss Flora (his grandmother) and Professor Jo (his mother) had let Sadie in on the family secret. What choice did they have? Sadie figured it out. But Beak said he was relieved that he had someone to talk to about it and that that someone was Sadie. Which made the soda-pop love mist inside Sadie's belly fizz even more.

Since then, they'd texted frequently and shared each other's locations on Trkr. She loved seeing a picture of his face move around the app's map as he roamed the Allendale campus, loved knowing where he was. Not because she was a stalker, but because it helped her feel connected to Beak when they were apart. There hadn't been any more school-approved occasions for the Charm House girls to hang out with the Allendale boys until this football game. And Sadie couldn't wait! She'd put in her earplugs, cozy up to Beak on the bleachers, share her popcorn, and captivate him with her new hair. Then, as if hearing her thoughts, he texted.

BEAK

I have a surprise. R U def going to the game tonight?

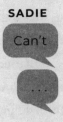

Sadie started sending the first part of her message, then got distracted by a vicious-sounding growl from the salon. She dashed next door to find Lindsey circling Val and Liv in the hallway—claws drawn, ready to pounce.

Taylor and Amy, both reptile-lights, didn't have the strength to pull a tiger away from two hyenas, but they had the smarts.

While Amy hissed warnings and gnashed her venomous fangs, Taylor, now invisible, was tying their shoelaces together.

"What's going on?" Sadie asked. Her voice was deep and commanding as if to say: *My hair may be pretty, but I'm tough.*

Lindsey lowered her claws. Another cat had arrived. She could relax. "These hyea*nerds* need to leave; that's what's going on."

"Speciest!" Val said.

"Come here and say that so I can scratch the freckles off that tragic face of yours." Lindsey lifted her gold nail file necklace, twisting the chain around her finger.

Val saw red when anyone made fun of her freckles and she lunged toward Lindsey. Not realizing that Taylor had tied her and Val's laces together, Liv jerked forward, smashed into Val, and they toppled to the floor.

Hilarious as it was, the Pack knew better than to waste this moment on a laugh. They were standing above their prey—the ultimate power position. They needed to stay serious.